AUTHOR	CLASS
HOYLE, F.	F
TITLE Westminster disaster	No. 478036569

THE WESTMINSTER DISASTER

THE
WESTMINSTER
DISASTER

FRED HOYLE
AND
GEOFFREY HOYLE

EDITED BY BARBARA HOYLE

HEINEMANN : LONDON

William Heinemann Ltd
15 Queen Street, Mayfair, London W1X 8BE

LONDON MELBOURNE TORONTO
JOHANNESBURG AUCKLAND

First published in Great Britain 1978
© 1978 by Fred Hoyle and Geoffrey Hoyle

434 34929 1

Printed Offset Litho and bound in Great Britain
by Cox & Wyman Ltd
London, Fakenham and Reading

Contents

The following characters, appearing in this story, have no relation to any persons known to the authors:

The President of the U.S.A.
The British Prime Minister
The Party Chairman

Heisal Woods, U.S. Secretary of State
Henry Fielding, British Home Secretary
Victor Kuzmin, Soviet Ambassador to the UN
Pamplin Forsythe, British Ambassador to the UN

Hermann Kapp, a terrorist
Anna Morgue (alias Félix), a terrorist
Abu l'Weifa (alias Pedro-the-Basque), a terrorist
Al Simmonds, a terrorist

Chief Inspector Cluny Robertson
Superintendent Willy Best
Sir Stanley Farrar, Commissioner of the Metropolitan Police

Robert Becker, head of the CIA
Valas Georgian, high official of the KGB
Igor Markov, subordinate to Valas Georgian
Colonel Barry Gwent, British Military Intelligence
General Holland, British Military Intelligence

Couriers:
  Alex Semjanov
  Captain Luri Otto
  Klaus Hartstein
  Father O'Donovan

  Sunion Webb, an intellectual
  Ernest Carruthers, an intellectual

Reporters:
  Jack Hart
  Stan Tambling

Agents:
  Robert Morales
  Rollie Schooners
  Maxwell Burt
  Ole Gröte
  Ron Weld

Tom Osborne, President of IHM of Canada
Roberta Osborne, his wife
Pieter van Elders, a minister of the South African government
David Kemp, a British lawyer
Paco Palmgren, a Swedish lawyer
Susi, a girl friend of Hermann Kapp
Jane Barrow, secretary to Becker
Colonel Abdul Hassim, a Libyan minister

Louis-le-Poisson

J. J. Marquette

Others, unnamed

The Threads

Just as a big river is formed by the confluence of many streams, so a massive affair like the Westminster Disaster was woven from many threads, threads which at first sight seemed separated from each other. It was while I was investigating one of the threads, connected with a Soviet agent called Morales, that I first met my wife. Her maiden name was Annette Osborne. Thereafter we continued the investigation together. It was an investigation with fragments in New York, Washington, South Africa, the Babushkin suburb of Moscow, and the very heart of London itself. We found an article in an Amsterdam newspaper telling of a light aircraft which crashed over the Dutch coast on the morning of the Westminster Disaster. It was this article that eventually led us to J. J. Marquette, a young West Indian pilot for a firm, Pengelly Charter, ostensibly in the business of giving tourists a flip over the sights of London. Of the three charred bodies found in the wreck of that lightplane, those of the two passengers interested us most—but of that more later. In view of the family connection, it is natural that we should take as the first thread Annette's own father.

Tom Osborne

It had been a beautiful day over the Lake of the Woods, near Sioux Narrows in the Ontario Province of Canada, with the water sparkling in the sunlight like untold millions of precious gems. As the evening shadows lengthened, Robert Morales silently and deftly changed his outer clothes for a skintight black outfit complete with hood. This he left rolled up on his forehead while he checked a waterproof bag containing photographic equipment. His companion, a heavyset man in a red check shirt, cut the outboard motor. With a grunt the man hauled the machine aboard, took up a paddle, and began with strong, measured strokes to propel the canoe toward the lakeshore.

Throughout the day, Robert Morales hadn't allowed his attention to wander for a moment. He and his companion had kept their quarry within view. With binoculars and the powerful outboard motor this had not been particularly difficult, because the quarry had scarcely troubled itself to move about. In fact, the two men in the other boat appeared to have spent most of the day placidly fishing. Yet through the binoculars Morales had seen them talking intently. A good place to talk, he had thought, out there on the water.

By now the heavyset man had brought the canoe close to the shore. Instead of seeking to land he paddled carefully and silently along the lakeside.

A mile away from the silently moving canoe, Pieter van Elders was putting the finishing touches to his toilet. After the day on the lake he had showered and dressed carefully, far more carefully than was necessary in this remote spot. He had done so to keep a check on his excitement, to force himself into a routine. He picked up the file of papers which lay there on the dressing table beside the mirror. He and Tom Osborne would be talking about the papers after dinner, putting finishing touches to the formalities of their agreement. Van Elders hesitated, and then put the file down. He would return for it once dinner was over, he decided.

If Pieter van Elders had been in Toronto or New York, he would never have left such sensitive documents lying exposed in his bedroom. In the extreme remoteness of the Lake of the Woods he left them simply because it would be inconvenient to be clutching the file throughout the informal dinner with his host and hostess.

Tom Osborne stood looking into the cheerful log fire. Except that his dark, slightly thinning hair was cut short, he looked more like the conductor of an orchestra than the president of International Heavy Metals of Canada. He had no illusions about the deal he was getting into with the South Africans. He knew there would be political trouble, certainly if this thing ever came out. But in his judgement as a mining executive with twenty-odd years of experience, the risk was worthwhile. Miners were always taking risks, sometimes big risks. What made the risk worthwhile was the simple overwhelming fact that the whole darned world would be running quite soon into one hell of a uranium shortage. IHM's own rich uranium deposit near Elliot Lake would be going thin by the nineteen nineties. So too would every other rich deposit, all over the world. In the long term much lower-grade ores would have to be used, and the biggest and most promising low-grade ores were in South Africa.

At this point in Tom Osborne's thinking, van Elders appeared. The talk over drinks was general and relaxed. The Osbornes were good hosts. Dinner was not delayed, and an excellent wine accompanied the best trout van Elders could remember.

Robert Morales waited in the darkness outside, watch-

ing until the three people inside reached the second
course of their meal. The window was open, and he could
hear their wine-warmed voices clearly through the bug
screen. The time had come for him to move. It took only
a moment for Morales to slip like a black shadow through
the house door and up the stairs. Swiftly and silently he
found the South African's bedroom. There all too obviously was a file of papers waiting to be fetched. Morales
took two exposures of each of the twenty-three sheets
of paper contained in the file. His camera was loaded
with ultra-high-speed film, and the bedroom light itself
gave him sufficient illumination. Each sheet took about
fifteen seconds, so that the whole file cost him no more
than six minutes. He spent a further few minutes searching for other papers. He found van Elders' diplomatic
passport, his ministerial identification, his wallet, travel-
ler's cheques, and airline ticket. Methodically he took
pictures of the passport and identification documents. Finally he checked that all the articles, the file particularly,
were just as he had found them.

He paused at the head of the stairs, for there were
noises of people moving below. Suddenly van Elders appeared, taking the stairs two at a time. Morales withdrew
into one of the other bedrooms and waited.

A moment later van Elders emerged from his bedroom
clutching the file firmly, and pounded rapidly down the
stairs. Robert Morales stood motionless, listening. Three
minutes. Five minutes. It was the woman he was alert
for now. No one came. In an instant he was down the
stairs. Once more he paused to listen. Satisfied that he
could hear the woman's voice, he stepped noiselessly out
of the house and on through the undergrowth to the
canoe, where the thickset man in the red check shirt
awaited him. As the canoe put silently out from the lake-

shore, Morales breathed deeply in the night air. His mission was complete.

That was on the evening of the 7th. Pieter van Elders left Sioux Narrows the following morning, satisfied that his job was well and truly done. He planned to take an evening flight to London, and thence to return immediately home to Johannesburg.

By the late afternoon of the 8th, phone calls reached Tom Osborne, from both Sudbury and Ottawa, informing him of political manoeuvres at the United Nations, manoeuvres affecting the proposed agreement between International Heavy Metals and the South Africans. The Canadian government was itself being asked for an explanation of the agreement. Osborne was consumed by an inner white-hot anger at the thought that a leak had occurred within IHM itself. Somebody in Sudbury, or Ottawa, had been talking, he decided, never suspecting that the information had actually been snatched from under his own nose. And even if he had entertained such a suspicion he would have dismissed it in the incorrect belief that an uproar at the United Nations could not have been stirred up so quickly.

Although he said nothing to his wife, Roberta Osborne knew that her husband was in a high old temper. She knew it from the tight-lipped way he was going about the house, and from his sudden decision to return to Sudbury.

The long drive to Sudbury, by way of Kenora, Thunder Bay, and Sault St. Marie, occupied the night of the 8th and the early morning of the 9th. Throughout the drive, Tom Osborne began to see, really for the first time, what a huge tiger he had gotten by the tail. It seemed like a small detail, to control the frequency of a laser to within

one or two parts in a million. But once you could do
that you could separate the isotopes of the heavy metals,
separate them far more easily than with the old centri-
fuge technique. Nobody was going to fuss very much
so long as your heavy metal was platinum or gadolinium
or mercury. But once your metal was uranium, the situation was different, because once you had separated out
the rare U-235, you could easily make nuclear bombs
from it. The technique, once you knew how, was actually
much less trouble than the older roundabout business
of making plutonium from U-238.

The huge tiger, of course, was the politics of Africa.
And standing behind the politics of Africa there was always the unremitting world struggle for oil, and for strategic materials of all kinds, materials like South African
chrome in which Tom Osborne had long wanted to gain
an interest. There were also diamonds, platinum, coal,
as well as the chrome, and, of course, the uranium itself.
The rocks of southern and central Africa, like those of
Canada, were old, and because of that they were rich
in mineral deposits of nearly every kind. The prize was
a glittering one, and it was now well within his grasp,
provided the political threat of the United Nations could
be overcome.

Of course there would be an uproar, because the capa-
bility of South Africa to separate U-235 would change
everything throughout the whole of Africa. There would
be no more cheap successes for the Marxists, not against
a South Africa equipped with easily made nuclear weapons. The Marxist route would lie elsewhere now, through
pressure at the UN, through pressure from the UN to
Ottawa.

It was Canadian government policy to appear to the
world like a thoroughly good fellow, anxious to do whatever was right, whatever "right" might be, and the UN

had become the self-appointed arbiter of that. For Canada, a country self-sufficient in almost everything—self-sufficient thanks to the farmers and to companies like IHM—it was a craven stupid policy. A policy, Osborne saw, that was going to be damned hard to change.

It took until the morning of the 10th to arrange an extraordinary meeting in Toronto of the Board of International Heavy Metals. The meeting was intended by Tom Osborne to inform the nonworking directors of the Board of the discussions with the Republic of South Africa. But even before the meeting could take place each of his directors received an anonymous, specially delivered letter, a letter describing with a fair amount of accuracy the general terms of the deal he had discussed with Pieter van Elders.

Nor was this the whole story. On the 9th, the stock of IHM had risen five whole points on the Toronto exchange. This rise had of course been due to heavy buying, which the IHM executive had traced to orders placed by Swiss banks. The sharp rise was still continuing, as Tom Osborne had just been informed by his secretary. Major movements in the price of a stock can be produced by the sudden purchase or sale of no more than a percent or two of all the shares outstanding. With seventy-one million shares of IHM outstanding, this implied a purchase of about a million and a half of them. At the present share price of about $40, the sum placed by the Swiss banks must therefore have been in the region of $60 million. A big sum for a private investor, or even for an institution, but not a big sum for a government, especially if that government happened to be a superpower.

The rise was big enough to encourage quite a number of other investors to sell, taking profit on their holdings of IHM stock. Indeed, brokers' reports showed that this

natural process was happening already. Eventually the
profit taking would become large enough to moderate
the rise. If at that point the big purchaser of a million
and a half shares were suddenly to unload on the market,
the price of IHM stock would plummet to well below
the price of $35 per share at which the whole exercise
had started. The price would be likely to fall even below
$25, and it would take some months to recover, because
investors generally would think something was badly
wrong with the stock, especially with the South African
deal under acute controversy at the UN. True, the foreign
government would lose some $20 million in the manoeu-
vre, but such a sum might be thought well spent if it
should cause IHM to call off the deal.

Tom Osborne began to address the meeting. Although
he forced himself to speak quietly, he found it impossible
to keep the smouldering rage out of his voice. He began
by saying that first and foremost he was a miner. He
said that although mining and politics were intertwined—
they had been so for thousands of years, since mining
first began—experience showed that miners did best if
they could manage to ignore the politics. For the good
reason that politics was short term and mining was long
term. A hot political potato today was often completely
forgotten tomorrow. Of course South Africa might be
different, but that was always said about every political
issue; it was always different. What was overwhelmingly
clear in this issue was that IHM could buy into the South
African mining scene at very little cost to itself. If South
Africa eventually went to the wall, very little would have
been lost.

A voice asked about the recent upswing of the IHM
share price. How much might eventually be lost due to
that? Nothing at all was Tom Osborne's answer. In fact,
there was money to be made in it. His proposal was that

IHM take advantage of a sharp downswing of the share price, should the anonymous purchaser decide to unload, by buying up the dumped stock, buying it into the company treasury. This would soon bring the share price back to the region of $35, and the anonymous purchaser's loss would become IHM's eventual gain, since the stock could be let out of treasury gradually, at the higher price.

Then Tom Osborne asked his directors to decide in their minds just how far they were prepared for their company to be pushed around. Did they really want their decisions to be made for them by politicians, not even by their own politicians in Ottawa, but by politicians in Moscow? Casting expediency aside, was there not a point at which a stand simply had to be made? Otherwise how far might the encroachment on their decision making go? As he spoke, his voice strengthened gradually, for he could detect from the subtle combination of small sounds—of his directors moving slightly in their seats, of their breathing even—that he was beginning to carry the meeting.

Another day passed in the life of Tom Osborne. It was just 9:30 A.M. on the morning of the 11th when he emerged from the midtown Hilton Hotel in Manhattan. He had come down from Toronto to New York the previous evening. He didn't quite know why he had come, for there was little he could do about the situation developing at the United Nations. It was really a matter of being close to the scene of the action.

Tom Osborne had arranged several business meetings, to give him the excuse to be there in New York, and it was toward the first such meeting that he was now heading. He thought of walking to his appointment, but then caught sight of a taxi standing some fifty yards away down the street. The taxi was apparently free, for its light was

on. Deciding he might not have quite sufficient time to
walk after all, Tom Osborne moved quickly toward the
taxi. Then he stopped because there was no driver to
be seen. His first instinct was to move closer. After a
few quick steps he stopped again, not quite knowing why,
or what caused the sudden prickling of the hairs on his
neck. A policeman strolled by the taxi, so surely everything had to be all right?

If the explosion had been a small one, Tom Osborne's
caution would have saved his life, but the explosion was
violent enough to cause a man standing more than a hundred yards away to be knocked down flat onto the sidewalk. A crowd assembled quickly around the crumpled
remains of the taxi and the rag-doll-like corpse of Tom
Osborne. Of the policeman there was nothing to be seen.

Moscow

Returning to August 8th, the day following the activities of Robert Morales, in one minute the Kremlin bells
would toll for 11:30 A.M. General Valas Georgian walked
the short distance that would bring him to the offices
of the Chairman. He was five feet ten inches in height,
deep of chest, and fifty-three years old. Which gave him
time, he often told himself, to wait until old age and
death swept away the thin crust of political authority
that still lay above him. Because he looked more formidable in uniform than in an ill-fitting, baggy suit, he always
wore his uniform on duty. His voice was powerful, with
rich overtones to it, as if he were a member of the Red
Army Choir—which indeed in his earlier years he had
actually been. Although the dark brown eyes were not
Mongolian in their slant, the face was big and rounded,
almost surely with a Siberian strain to it.

Valas Georgian was now a high-ranking KGB officer,

but he still continued to emphasise his earlier connexion with the regular army. He did so in simple, practical ways rather than by open statement, such as always turning up for a meeting precisely at the agreed time, to within the last second or two. So it was that he now walked into the Chairman's suite exactly at 11:30 A.M. The Chairman rose to greet him. Then the two of them settled back in comfortable chairs, a low table between them carrying two small glasses, a decanter of vodka, and a slender blue file.

Even granted the efficiency of the Soviet intelligence machine, of its external tentacles and of its home-based analytical offices, it was remarkable that the papers photographed by Robert Morales in Canada only eight hours before could have been processed already and acted upon. The credit for this swift response fell largely to Georgian himself. Every morning, seven days a week, he took extreme care to arrive at eight o'clock sharp at his office, just like a piece of precision machinery. On his desk there would be a mountain of papers, telegrams, interoffice memos, reports, and papers of state. To have read the lot in detail would have been an impossible task. Each day would have brought a backlog of unfinished material, so that within a month his office would have become unmanageable and his job impossible. Instead, he skimmed through the papers, and it was in the skill with which he did so that Georgian had established himself as a driving force within the Soviet hierarchy. By 10 A.M. each day he had picked out the two or three most important matters to which he would give his own personal attention. The rest of the material was then gathered up by his secretary and distributed for action among his assistants. On this day he had quickly seized on the Canadian information. He had come on it about 9:15 A.M., and had immediately referred it to the Chairman himself.

Now, by 11:30 A.M., the Chairman had conferred with
his Politburo members and action had already been
agreed.

The action was straightforward enough, as Valas Georgian had known it would be. It took the Chairman only
a few moments of explanation, and the future course to
be taken was agreed between the two men, almost as
if it were a matter of routine only. Then the Chairman
busied himself with the glasses and decanter, and they
toasted their decision with a quick snap.

By the evening of the 10th, Valas Georgian was once
again back in the Chairman's offices. He was gratified
on this second visit to have attended an emergency meeting of the Security Subcommittee of the Politburo. By
then the actions agreed to on the 8th had of course been
taken, actions in South Africa and at the United Nations.
The question of sanctions against South Africa would be
coming before the Security Council. The problem now
to be considered by the Politburo was whether a veto
against such a motion might be cast by the British. Papers
to that effect had just come in from an agent of proven
reliability in Washington, D.C.

Georgian had been asked for an estimation of the British Prime Minister, and he had replied that there was
no reliable "vector" on the man, which meant that the
Prime Minister's actions were not considered predictable.
It had been decided that Georgian should implement
measures to cause the British to desist—measures quite
independent of any diplomatic pressure on the Americans.

The Head of Action Operations-European had been
summoned from his home and was already waiting when
Valas Georgian reached his office. Igor Markov was a
sandy-haired, freckle-faced man with a snub nose, an ob-

vious peasant type like the Chairman himself. But
whereas the Chairman was crafty, Markov was subtle.
If Georgian had not been a decade older, and on a signifi-
cantly higher rung of the party ladder, he would have
feared the subtlety of Igor Markov. It took remarkably
little time to explain to him exactly what was wanted,
and to make it clearly understood that the Russian Embassy in London was not to become overtly involved.
Nor must anything be done which might negate the diplomatic pressure to be put upon the Americans. It all
had to be executed in an untraceable fashion, whatever
it was that Markov might decide to do. The sandy-haired
man assured his booming, full-voiced chief that he had
entirely understood. Calmly he rose to leave, saying that
the stated conditions would be carefully obeyed. Valas
Georgian thought of offering a valedictory nip to his visitor, but then resisted, although he would not have been
averse to a glass himself. Such a gesture would be remembered, perhaps to be brought out against him at a future
time. So he conducted Markov from his office in a proper,
formal style, satisfied that he himself had made a good
showing that night.

Igor Markov was driven by his chauffeur to the headquarters of his group, headquarters located in the northern Babushkin suburb of Moscow. The breathtaking scope
of the problem before him was without precedent in his
experience. He would be working on it through the night,
building a great flow chart of events in his mind. He
had six days to perfect and execute some grand plan.
In six days there were one hundred forty-four hours.
Much could happen in a single minute, and in one hundred forty-four hours there were eight thousand, six hundred and forty minutes. Critical events could even take
place in a second or less, and in six days there were five
hundred and eighteen thousand, four hundred seconds.

Much time was therefore available, provided only that the plan was correctly conceived.

Washington and London

The third of the threads running between the 7th and 11th of August involved politics at a very high level, both in Britain and the United States. Already at 10:30 A.M. on the 9th, Heisal Woods, Secretary of State, entered the President's office, the office with the oval shape which had won quite as much popular notice as any of the actual decisions taken within it.

Woods was a five-foot-eight ball of intense energy. His hair was greying now, but his face had the healthy glow of a onetime athlete. It annoyed him that he was latterly reduced to wearing eyeglasses. He had a fund of genuinely funny stories and consequently was always much in demand as a speaker. Naturally equipped with such qualities, and a lawyer by training, he had never experienced difficulty with the committees of Congress, which made him an outstandingly valuable member of the Cabinet, so giving him easy access to the President.

Probably if he hadn't enjoyed such easy access to the President he would not have reported the situation brewing in New York quite so soon. He would have delayed until the afternoon meeting of the General Assembly of the UN was over. But Heisal Woods had a bad feeling about this situation. It was just a bit too quick, a bit too obviously orchestrated for his own liking.

"So what, we've had sanctions against South Africa before," the President remarked when Woods had said his piece. The President was a tough-looking bald man in his early fifties, a year or two older than Woods himself. Although he was convivial, sociable, and relaxed in the evenings, the President was always razor sharp at this time in the morning. But he was still feeling his way with a wise caution, having only succeeded to his exalted office in January of that year. His remark to Heisal Woods meant that he was now looking for information. The last UN motion for sanctions against South Africa had been before his time. The American veto had been used on that occasion.

"'We're in a short-hairs situation," Woods began.

The President got up from his desk. "How come?" he asked, biting the end off a cigar with his strong front teeth.

"We can neither afford to allow sanctions to be passed nor can we afford to use the veto to stop it," Woods went on.

The President blew a cloud of smoke. He could readily see why using the veto would be awkward, awkward for him personally, because the black vote had been critically important in his winning the preceding November's race. The black vote did not love South Africa. He also had a fair idea of why the United States could not afford to have sanctions actually passed against South Africa, but he waited for the Secretary of State to speak, hoping that Woods would have an "out" from the dilemma.

"And another thing," the Secretary went on, "it gets harder all the time to use the veto. And all the time it gets more necessary to do so. Sort of contradictory."

"How's that?" the President grunted again.

"More necessary, because our oil imports from the Middle East are increasing all the time."

"We must do something about that," the President scowled, blowing out another cloud of smoke.

"A lot of people have tried, without too much success. And besides the oil, there's the chrome. If we lose South African chrome we're in hock to the Soviets straight-away."

"It's all the pressure from within that's the devil," the President agreed.

"Which the Soviets know about. It's an easy orchestration for them."

"So what do you suggest? Let's have your plan, Mr. Secretary."

"Maybe I haven't a plan."

"You'd better. It's your job." By now the President's cigar had gone out, but it still remained clamped between his teeth.

Before replying, Woods went over to a side table where there was a small coffee urn. He poured himself a cup, added two sugar lumps, and stirred in a modest quantity of cream.

"Nothing can actually be done by the United Nations General Assembly, of course. The General Assembly can only make a recommendation to the Security Council. But when the sanctions motion is made in the Security Council the veto must be cast, except we mustn't cast it. The plan is as simple as that," Woods explained as he walked with the cup back to his chair.

The President nodded slowly. "So . . . ?"

"We must fix it for the British to do the job," Woods continued. "Every argument I can think of goes that way. The British have much less of a colour problem than we have, three to four hundred percent less of a problem. Their North Sea oil is coming in now, flooding in. Besides, they have their own people in South Africa, and . . ."

"Right, right, I can see all that. But what's the *quid pro quo?*"

"Quids, literally. Help with the debts the British piled up in the seventies."

"You think they'll play?"

"Yes." Woods emphasised his answer with a firm nod.

"Well, if you've got it all so tidily worked out, why

trouble me with it?" The President had known all along that Heisal Woods had something else on his mind, something besides this veto business.

"Well, why so sudden? Why so quick? Why jump over the candlestick? What would make the Soviets pull out all the stops? Why just now?" Woods asked as he finished his coffee.

For answer, the President took a file from a desk drawer. He handed it to Woods, saying, "Just came in. I've hardly had a chance to read it myself. It looks important."

The President took another cigar out of a case which lay on the desk top. He tapped it vigorously against the desk and slowly lit it as he watched the gathering scowl on his Secretary's face.

"Compulsive reading," Woods said at last. "Do we have this laser thing?" he asked, seemingly as an afterthought.

"We're working on it. I imagine a lot of people are working on it."

"But how come the Canadians . . ."

"My scientific advisers tell me these high-technology things are capricious. You try the obvious and straightforward idea, and what happens—nothing. Somebody else tries a crazy idea, and it works. That's what seems to have happened."

"With International Heavy Metals? Of course they're a big corporation," Woods nodded reflectively.

"So International Heavy Metals have something which they're preparing to pass on to the South Africans. Put yourself in the Soviet position, Mr. Secretary. How would you go about stopping the deal?"

"I'd do just what they seem to be doing. I'd get sanctions passed by the UN against South Africa."

"And why?"

"Because that would be the only thing that could make

the Canadian government apply the chopper to the deal."

"So sanctions would really stop it?" the President repeated, staring intently at Woods.

"It would, Mr. President, it surely would. The Canadians have always been very pliant to world opinion."

"So you have the answer to your question?"

"I guess so."

"Do you want to change your idea, of getting the British to apply the brakes?"

"No."

"You know what you're doing? Forgive the question."

Heisal Woods sat for a moment.

"Yes," he said eventually, "I reckon I know what I'm doing."

"No point in speaking to the French?"

"Not really. The French will go the way they want to go. Maybe they will use the veto. Maybe they won't. We can't depend on it." Woods sat for a moment, grinning ruefully.

"Strange people," the President nodded in agreement.

The ultimate election-winning politician was the British Prime Minister. He had a round benign face. His thin-rimmed spectacles softened his eyes, as spectacles always do, so that on television he appeared as a kindly, overindulgent father figure. His hair had not worn thin. It stood up well, about an inch and a half from the skull in tight curls, giving him a friendly golliwog appearance. He spoke quietly with seeming total sincerity, quite unlike the unctuous manner of his predecessors in office. But behind the benign face, behind the friendly eyes, behind the quiet voice, was a sharp scheming brain. Yet this was hard to know, because the Prime Minister's ultimate political artistry lay in a total concealment of that brain, a concealment just as complete as that which he afforded to his private parts.

On the evening of August 10th he listened to two impassioned harangues, one from the Chancellor, the other from the Foreign Secretary. The Foreign Secretary spoke of the paramount need to maintain respect for Britain in the eyes of the world. He detailed the decline of moral standing that would flow from a veto cast against the South African motion in the forthcoming Security Council meeting. The Chancellor, on the other hand, argued with equal emphasis, if not with equal fervour, in favour of accepting the deal offered by the American government. He emphasised how much more readily the British economy would then pass from rough water to smooth. And throughout his argument the P.M. just sat there on the other side of his desk, tapping his fingers and looking like a benign Buddha. It was a performance that always unnerved the Chancellor. Even though he had worked with the Prime Minister for many years, and had won a fair share of the arguments, the Chancellor always felt he wasn't "getting through." John Boddington, the Foreign Secretary, felt better, though. The seraphic face of the Prime Minister, the dignity of the nodding head, the encouraging smile, all went to convince him that his case was fully understood and accepted.

Actually the Prime Minister was thinking that "poor John" would definitely have to go in the next Cabinet reshuffle. Or still better, possibly he could be persuaded to resign over this particular issue. With the greatly increased flow of oil from the North Sea, the pathetic begging-bowl kind of image which "poor John" insisted on cutting in the eyes of the world was becoming more of a liability than an advantage to the government.

The American deal would mean somewhere between

three and five pounds more in the average weekly pay
packet. It was a good working rule that any sudden in-
crease in the pay packet would produce a voter swing
of one percent for every pound sterling. The Prime Minister's own calculations suggested at least a three percent
swing, sufficient to change an electoral stalemate into a
landslide.

New York, the United Nations

On August 9th, less than twenty-four hours after the
activities of Robert Morales, there was action at the
United Nations. The New York police were doing their
usual job of controlling the press of traffic around the
UN building in the late afternoon of August 9th. The
job was no sinecure because of the need to give the every-
day traffic, upon which the welfare of the city depended,
proper access to the East River Drive. It was a job the
police did not like, because of the difficulty of separating
bona fide UN delegates from all the swingers and hangers-
on. To be plain too, the whole thing was a cross which
the city had to bear.

Victor Kuzmin, Soviet Ambassador to the United Nations, was one of the last to enter the hall of the General
Assembly with its colorful display of the flags of member
nations. He nodded and occasionally lifted an arm in recognition of the delegates of Third World countries. Then
he took his seat, conferred briefly with the man on his
right, put on the headphones, and slewed around toward
the chair, as if to indicate that he was ready for the meeting to begin.

Kuzmin knew the meeting of the General Assembly
would end with an overwhelming vote of recommendation to the Security Council that sanctions be imposed
against South Africa, on the ground that South Africa

had failed to "perform the obligations incumbent upon it" under a judgement of the International Court of Justice. Only a few Western nations would probably abstain as they had done on previous occasions when a similar motion had been passed. There would be no drama in the vote; the result was a foregone conclusion. Indeed, the Soviet Union could arrange such a vote in the General Assembly at any time it chose.

The drama lay elsewhere. It lay with France, Britain, and the United States, the three who could veto the motion after it was referred to the Security Council. The problem for the Soviet Union lay in forcing these three countries into acting against their own best interests. The key to the United States position lay in the black situation which Kuzmin knew to be under orchestration in South Africa. This could be relied on to inflame black opinion in the United States, and so to put irresistible pressure on the President, and hence on the State Department. Nor were the French difficult. All that need be done with the French was to appeal to their material self-interest. Kuzmin listened as the principal delegate from Kuwait rose to speak. The French would not go against an Arab proposal. So much had been obvious, and this was exactly why Kuzmin had been at pains to arrange that the first motion against South Africa should come from an Arab source. He allowed himself to wonder within his own mind, having passed lunchtime in convivial fashion, why the Arabs were so gullible. Once the southern tip of Africa had been sealed off, the oil states of the Persian Gulf would fall like so many overripe plums. Yet here was this Kuwaiti busily proposing the very motion that would bring on his own downfall. Israel was the key, of course. Waving Israel in front of Arab eyes still paid off handsomely. This was an easy part of the game, and so were the French, Kuzmin congratulated himself.

This left the British, the seedy British, the lords of yes-
teryear. Kuzmin drummed his fingers on the table as
he looked across at the British delegation, at the delegation leader, Pamplin Forsythe, a sagged waxwork of a
man. Something drastic had better be done about the
British, Victor Kuzmin decided, something they would
not easily forget. The alcohol in his blood caused him
to smile broadly at the thought.

By the afternoon of August 11th the sanctions motion
had moved from the General Assembly to the Security
Council. By then there had been discussions both in
Washington and London. There had been a "conversation" between Washington and London, a conversation
that had been "learned of" by the Kremlin.

Pamplin Forsythe made his way that afternoon, head
down, creeping like Shakespeare's snail of a schoolboy,
toward the United Nations building. He had decided to
walk because the longer he delayed the journey, the better. On his first day at public school somebody had called
him "pig-face," and then the whole class of new boys
had taken up the chant of "pig-face." Right from that
time he had been acutely sensitive about his relation to
society. And the casting of this bloody awful veto would
earn him worse names than "pig-face." It would put him
right outside the pale of decent New York society. The
sooner he moved from his job at the UN, the better that
would be too, he thought miserably to himself. For this
job you needed nerves of steel and a face of brass, just
like the bloody Russians.

In spite of his seemingly wayward progress through
the New York streets, Forsythe arrived in the Security
Council chamber at just about the right time. He felt
calmer about it now, glad almost that it would soon be
over and done with. He had just about time to confer

with his staff, and to check that all his papers were in proper order in relation to the agenda, when the President called the meeting to order.

It took three-quarters of an hour to reach the main item of business, yesterday's recommendation of the General Assembly that sanctions be imposed forthwith against South Africa. Pamplin Forsythe would have been hard pressed to recall the business of that first three-quarters of an hour. The early business simply rippled over his head, as he thought through and through the precise form of the sentences in which he would announce the British veto.

The moment of crisis came at last, as it invariably does. The President moved to the critical item, beginning by describing briefly the events which had occurred in the General Assembly on the previous day. Pamplin Forsythe glanced across the chamber at the Russian delegation, for Victor Kuzmin had his arm raised. Then, not content to wait to be noticed, Kuzmin began to wave his arm, demanding attention. Forsythe guessed that the South African riot and killings of the preceding day must have decided the Russian to lead the debate instead of leaving the matter to the Swedes. Wearily, as Kuzmin rose to speak, he set himself to listen to the translator.

For a moment he thought the translator must be getting it wrong. It was only when Kuzmin ended quickly and resumed his seat that Forsythe really believed the words he had just heard through the headphones. The Russians had asked for a week's postponement of the debate. Even in the relief which flooded miraculously through his being, Pamplin Forsythe found himself wondering how the Soviets would make use of the coming week. It would be in some kind of offensive against the use of the veto. Doubtless, but what? He decided the Russian tactics would be to put on pressure to persuade

the Americans not to do a deal with the British. Then
he himself would be off the hook. He left the chamber
feeling like a criminal reprieved.

South Africa

The earliest Russian move in South Africa itself was
in evidence already by the evening of the 8th. In the
gathering darkness Rollie Schooners drove his VW Golf
along Coen Steytler to its junction with Table Bay Boulevard in Cape Town. He crossed the traffic there, so as
to get into Dock Road. Nearing the corner with Ebenezer
Street, he came to a gentle stop and waited.

It was several minutes before an apparent passerby
came toward the car. Schooners rolled down the window
on the passenger side of the car. A black face topped
by a woollen cap appeared in the open space.

"You got the time, mister?" was the question.

"Six-thirty," Schooners answered without troubling to
look at his watch.

"Time for a man to think about his future."

Satisfied that this indeed was his contact, Schooners
unlocked the door, and the black immediately slipped
into the car.

For the next few moments there would be some danger, and Schooners had no liking for danger. He was well
paid by a Soviet-penetrated commercial company for or-
ganizing the storage of a particular commodity. The commodity was brought into port quite openly, with the
proper duty paid to customs. A few crates would then
be diverted to Schooners for illicit storage. He had several
deposits, and each one he had built up with care. Now
he was going to lose a deposit but that also was planned.

Schooners drove his passenger deeper still into the
dockland area. The fellow talked far too much, and with

an American accent, which explained his cockiness. It
also made Schooners still more nervous, since he had
no wish at all to be stopped by the police. He parked
about two hundred yards away from the small warehouse
where the crates were hidden under a pile of scrap metal,
hidden in a false bottom of the ground floor. He led the
way along ill-lit narrow passageways, arriving a couple
of minutes later at a darkened courtyard. With a gloved
hand he fumbled for the old-fashioned key and opened
the big wooden door which gave onto the yard. He told
his companion that the stuff was under the floor, and
left the man to it. Moments later he had his car turned
back toward Dock Road. Satisfied he was not being followed, Schooners reached the well-lit Table Bay Boulevard again. Instead of recrossing it, he turned left along
it, with a welcome warmth suffusing his plump thirty-
year-old frame. He was rid of the warehouse now, with
its hidden seventy-odd crates of whiskey. There was nothing to connect him with the place—he'd made sure of
that. All that remained was for him to enjoy a well-earned
dinner.

The name of Schooners' contact was Maxwell Burt.
Burt had been born within a hundred yards of the inter-
section of 116th Street and Lenox Avenue, in the Harlem
district of Manhattan. An observer twenty years ago of
Burt at play in the streets off Lenox would have noted
the same strength and aggression in him which made
outstanding football and baseball players from so many
of his contemporaries. But Maxwell Burt had a character
different from those contemporaries, a character that
could not withstand the early disappointments which be-
set every young athlete.
For another thing, his natural appetite for girls was
not to be in any way sublimated to athleticism. Because

he needed money as well as girls, he had begun with simple muggings, from the bushes which are so conveniently provided for such a purpose in Central Park. At first he had splashed the money around to get the girls he wanted. Then he had found it better to take the girls he wanted simply by rape. It was much less expensive that way. Rape brought a change in his tastes, from black girls to white. He had made the change in the first place because white girls found it harder to identify a coloured man afterward. And then he had grown to like that way, because it gratified him both physically and mentally, mentally because of the girls' being white.

By his mid-twenties Maxwell Burt dropped out of mugging, however. Mugging was too dangerous for what it achieved, and there were much better pickings elsewhere, especially in politics because of the reverse colour prejudice that was developing strongly throughout the United States. Partly by subtlety, partly by brashness, partly by intimidation, he contrived to get himself elected to Congress as the representative of one of the tough uptown Manhattan districts. Then he had two mighty good years in Washington, until his financial manipulations brought him to the point of exposure. At that point it became expedient for him to quit the United States.

From the United States he had moved into the twilit territory of international sharp practice, close to the edge of crime the whole while. It was at that point that he was noticed by several intelligence agencies, including the CIA. But it was eventually to Moscow that Burt had turned. It was in Moscow that he had graduated from an ill-directed amateur into a skilled professional. The KGB had put considerable effort and priority on him, because there were many places in the world, Africa especially, where a carefully trained American-born black could be exceedingly effective.

A day and a half later, early on the morning of the 10th, Maxwell Burt had moved the scene of his operations to Johannesburg. There were six of them in the dingy room where they had spent the night, three young coloured lads of about twenty, two whites, and Burt himself. The whites had dressed themselves in police uniforms, and they were now carefully checking two 30.06 hunting rifles. It was time for them all to be moving. The three coloured lads left first, then the two whites. Maxwell Burt himself stayed on alone for a further few moments, making sure—as he had been taught to do—that nothing was being left behind that would give an indication of their identity. His last move was to check his Smith and Wesson pistol until he was satisfied with its functioning. With the weapon concealed on his person, Burt made his way down a narrow flight of stairs into an alley, to begin a two-mile walk to his contact, a taxi driver whom he would meet close by the Anglican cathedral. There was some danger for an armed coloured man to be walking the streets, but Maxwell Burt knew the police would be having plenty of trouble on their hands for the next hour or two.

The crates of whiskey which had appeared during the early hours of the morning in the black township of Soweto had done their inevitable work. Chanting crowds of youths surged along the roads from the southwest into Johannesburg. It had started individual fights, and more serious fights between gangs of students and groups of immigrant workers. The authorities at BOSS were not particularly surprised by these events, for they were well used to riots being timed to occur at critical moments of international tension.

Police squads equipped with helmets and shields and with canisters of tear gas had already been dispatched

to Soweto with strict orders to contain the riot there without gunfire. The roving crowds of youths moving toward
the city had been allowed to continue, because the police
now understood that these youths were being used as
bait to occupy their attention and to fill the jails with
prisoners who would turn out later to have no close connexion with the real organisers of the riot.

The chief of police was relieved to find that the reports
before him showed no unusual accumulation of blacks
within the city proper. But the police reports said nothing
of some two score trained black operatives who had di-
vided themselves into ten or more small groups. Since
these groups were distributed over a square mile of the
Johannesburg downtown area, there had indeed been
very little for the police to notice.

What followed was easily noticed, however. A girl teller
of the Netherlands Bank collapsed with a thin terrifying
wail on the steps of the bank itself. Scarcely anybody
had seen the flash of a knife blade, but they noticed the
girl as her life ebbed swiftly away. A stock jobber on
his way to Hollard Street was buying cigarettes in a tobac-
conist's. He had just time to turn around as a lead-inlaid
brick followed by a petrol bomb burst through the main
display window of the shop. He was permitted but a moment of confused thought before flames burst everywhere around him.

A dozen acts of sudden violence were reported to the
chief of police. They came so precipitately one upon another that his natural impulse was to believe he had made
a grievous blunder. He overreacted by committing extensive police squads to the scenes of violence, and he gave
orders for men to be moved back from Soweto.

The police officers in charge at Soweto were in some
considerable confusion and so thought nothing when a

car, seemingly containing two of their own men, passed through the cordon they had been using to contain the crowd. A thrown rock shattered the windscreen of the car, which continued on its way, apparently half out of control, until it stopped at a point somewhat distant from both the police and the rioting crowds. A truck rambled toward the car, and as it passed slowly by, two whites in police uniform were able to emerge unnoticed from the car. They carried 30.06 hunting rifles with telescopic attachments. Losing little time, they had sought shelter in a nearby house with broken windows. It took a moment or two to take up suitable positions at the windows, and to let drug tablets steady down their heartbeats. Then the two men fired the first shots. Both were marksmen, and in the next five seconds each fired four rounds into the crowd of shouting blacks. Five seconds more and they were on their way, to the second stage of their planned assignment.

Maxwell Burt sat at the wheel of the taxi which he had taken over from his contact. It was still the morning rush hour in downtown Johannesburg and twice somebody had tried to hire him, but each time he had grunted hoarsely and pointed to the ticking meter. Eventually a porter at the Jan Smuts Hotel gave him the signal he was waiting for. Flicking off the meter, he drove to the hotel door. The porter opened the rear door of the cab and the three men got in. He had been expecting only two, one French, the other English. The third spoke with an American accent which could only make a good situation even better. They asked if he would drive them to Soweto, as indeed he knew they would.

It was also inevitable that the taxi would be stopped on its way to Soweto. Burt's passengers flashed their identification cards at the police officer who intercepted them.

Thinking that to let accredited reporters continue would
be the lesser of two evils, the officer allowed them to
proceed.

On the outskirts of the black township, Maxwell Burt
stopped the taxi. He explained that he wasn't risking damage to his vehicle, but that he would go with them on
foot to the police cordon. This seemed reasonable to the
reporters, and they willingly followed as Burt led them
toward the distant uproar. Helliwell Sutcliffe of the
Washington Post was distracted by the uproar, otherwise
he would have been more curious about the intonations
in Burt's speech. It was ticking away in his subconscious
that something was amiss, but he had not yet analysed
his unease at the moment the bullet hit him.

The marksmen with the 30.06 rifles had expected there
to be two targets. Instead they found three. The white
men with the rifles distinguished their quarries from Maxwell Burt by the fact that their victims were white. Their
bullets brought death instantly for Helliwell Sutcliffe but
not for Bill Lomax of the London *Times* or for Roger
Demonies of the Paris *Le Monde*. Since Burt had no time
to wait while the two wounded men died, he dispatched
them quickly with the Smith and Wesson pistol. All that
now remained was for the bodies of the three reporters
to be found close to the scene of the riots. This would
be done within the hour. Then Maxwell Burt's assignment
as a onetime agent in South Africa would be completed.

The Threads Interweave

It will be apparent that the threads so far developed were interwoven from the beginning. Yet to August 11th it was possible, for the sake of clarity, to present them separately. From the 12th onward, however, separation becomes impracticable. From there, it is essential to describe events in the strict chronological order in which they occurred. August 12th marked the beginning of the implementation of the plan of Igor Markov, a plan designed to prevent the casting of a United Nations veto by the British government. The plan called for a cast of couriers, of agents, of fellow travellers, of terrorists—a grey-hued cast very different from the higher echelons of government which had mainly occupied the stage until this point.

Moscow, Early Morning

Sunion Webb was surprised to be awakened in his bed at the newly reconstructed Rossiya Hotel by two men wearing cloth caps. He dressed hurriedly, once he had learned that the Soviet authorities wished to consult him on a matter of great urgency. Much as he was used to

the sudden shifts of mood of the Russians, he was surprised further when one of the men insisted that he
should pack his bag and take that along too. Until that
moment he had thought himself to be enjoying an ex-
tended visit to Moscow and to the Soviet Union generally,
with little urgency in his movements. Indeed, a relaxed
attitude to the pace of events was essential to appreciate
Russia and its people, as Sunion Webb had discovered
long ago.

Sunion had been so named by a classically educated
father. His father had inherited a textile business in Dar-
lington, England, just before the First World War. At
another time his father would probably have sold the
business, since he held the liberal views of the early twen-
tieth century, views dominated by the doctrine that capitalist industry was the root of all evil. But the coming
of war had caused his father to operate the business himself, and such were the profitable noncompetitive conditions of the time that the business prospered greatly, to
the considerable economic advantage of the family.

Throughout Sunion's youth, during the nineteen twenties, his father had continued to maintain a liberal posture, veering toward socialism. It was a posture with a
strong thread of hypocrisy in it, the hypocrisy which expressed concern for the "working man," while living comfortably itself in an upper-class style. Although he had
never admitted openly to it, his father had been intelli-
gent enough to be aware of this inconsistency. He was
also conscious of how comfortably he himself had been
sheltered through the war years while so many other
men of his own age were being ruthlessly slaughtered
on the battlefields of France and Flanders. These two
strands of inner self-doubt had generated within his father a deep sense of guilt which prevented him from
enjoying his particularly good fortune, and which had

hung like a cloud upon the household during Sunion's
formative years.

Sunion's mother had been an ardent suffragette. She
was a woman of strong character, stronger than the father. Sunion had either inherited his mother's firmness
or he had learned to imitate it as he had grown older,
to the point where he had entered the University of Cam-
bridge as a fiery young socialist. He had read history,
economics, and law, and he had debated social issues with
unabated enthusiasm at the Union. The time was the
late nineteen twenties, just when the capitalist world was
struck down by the Great Depression. Sunion Webb had
been an able student, taking "firsts" in each of the two
parts of his Tripos. He was fully conversant now with
the writings of Marx, Engels, and Lenin. To him, the
Great Depression seemed the confirmation, the proof,
of all his socialist studies.

With his natural intelligence, upbringing, and educa-
tion, Sunion Webb might have seemed destined to
emerge as a socialist leader, perhaps to emerge as a considerable political figure in the rise to dominance of the
British Labour party. When in the years immediately following the Second World War he was elected the parliamentary member for an industrial town in the southwest,
this scenario did indeed seem on its way to realisation.
But Sunion Webb did not attain even junior ministerial
rank in the government. There were several contributory
reasons for his failure to advance in the Labour hierarchy,
but the fundamental one was simply that he had no genuine affinity for the workingmen he claimed so strenuously
to represent. Others of the intellectual left wing took
trouble to hide carefully this same inconsistency in their
positions, but not Sunion Webb. He came to dislike the
opportunism of his own leaders, whom he felt to be flirt-
ing with capitalists and capitalism in a quite unacceptable

way. He convinced himself that the mantle of true socialism had descended on his own shoulders, and his speeches
came more and more to reflect this opinion. The process
was cumulative, with Sunion Webb moving ever more
closely to a doctrinaire Marxist position. When in the
late nineteen fifties he lost his parliamentary seat to a
Conservative opponent, his estrangement from the Labour party was too great, the intellectual chasm too wide,
for reconciliation to be deemed possible by either the
party leaders or by Sunion Webb himself.

His move toward the Communist position was then
decisive and complete. He accepted the Russian interven-
tions, first in Hungary, and later in Czechoslovakia, as
necessary for the preservation of true socialism. He came
also to accept the need for world revolution, the need
to overthrow the capitalist system by force, since otherwise the insidious influence of capitalism would never
be suppressed. True, Russian actions were sometimes
harsh, but the world itself was a harsh place, and the
ends justified the means.

Before 1960 Sunion Webb had visited the USSR on a
number of occasions, but only sporadically, not regularly
as in the years following 1960. He travelled now at Soviet
expense, seeing himself as a political consultant, as scien-
tists and engineers might see themselves as technical con-
sultants. And from time to time he visited Third World
countries to confer with the people there on Soviet behalf. For these trips, which he enjoyed, he was well paid,
so that it was a case of combining business with pleasure—
although Sunion Webb himself would not have thought
about it in such an overt capitalist way.

He was a small man, five feet six inches in height, with
a mane of white hair combed back from the forehead.
His nose was small and shapely, like a woman's, and his
fair-skinned complexion remained good, even in his sixty-

third year. The hat and cape which he wore were reminiscent of Lloyd George, an echo from the past which he carefully emphasised by the growth of a suitably shaped moustache. It was in this style that he emerged from his room at the Rossiya, bag in hand, to join the two men who had called on him so unexpectedly. He was thoroughly proficient in the Russian language and had no difficulty understanding what the men had told him, namely that a matter of some urgency had arisen on which his advice was needed, and that a car was waiting at the hotel door.

The car took him from near the Moskva River in a northerly direction, via Chernyshevsky Street to the Garden Ring, and thence along Mir Avenue. Past Dzerzhinsky Park the vehicle continued for some way into the suburb of Babushkin, and then came to a stop in a sheltered court. The houses surrounding the court appeared at first sight to be residential, but Sunion Webb realised at second glance that the whole area had been converted for official purposes. He was immediately escorted into the buildings, which, being several houses connected together by corridors and stairs, were somewhat complex in their internal structure Two or three moments later he was in the office of a sandy-haired, freckle-faced man, who introduced himself as Igor Markov.

Igor Markov had sweated in his shirt sleeves through the humid August night. He had first formulated a general plan for persuading the British to desist from the casting of a veto, filling in the details later, and so by morning he had arrived at an extensive flow chart of projected events. At first he had given numerical symbols to the operators on the chart, but then with the chart in good shape he had begun to compile a master list, relating the numerical symbols to the code designations of actual human agents. Through this further stage of the work he had consulted intelligence files on many individuals, files that were stored in a master computer program.

A key operative who knew England well, preferably an Englishman, was certainly needed, a person who could move openly without serious suspicion, a person to whom money could be trusted, a person who was administratively responsible, above all, a person who would not become squeamish under pressure. Although no special technical expertise would be needed in this person, the requirements were certainly not commonplace. A computer search had thrown up only a few operatives with proper matching qualifications. Of these few, Igor Markov's first choice would have been an individual now living in an expensive villa within easy earshot of the cannon that is fired always at midday on the Gianicolo in Rome. But it would have offended Markov's basic principles to transmit instructions to a key operative by radio. He wanted the man sitting there before him in his own office. He wanted to watch the man's face as the broad features of the plan were explained to him. He wanted to watch for telltale signs of doubt or of revulsion. And getting his favoured man from Rome to Moscow would consume one of the precious six days available to him, which was not to be thought of, unless a satisfactory quicker alternative could not be found. According to the computer a satisfactory quicker alternative might be found, at no greater distance than the Rossiya Hotel.

It was unnecessary for Igor Markov to explain the full details of the flow chart to Sunion Webb. There were three parts of it that were essential, however, and these he explained carefully, twice over. Webb found the proposal both astonishing and fearsome. But considering the shameful character of the proposed British veto at the United Nations, which Markov also explained to him, he thought the proposal justified. He felt this in his own mind, not because he was persuaded to think so. Indeed, Igor Markov was exceedingly careful to avoid persuasion of any kind.

It took Sunion Webb fully half an hour to grasp the enormous magnitude of the plan. When he had done so, he asked a number of clear-cut operational questions, which Markov then went on to answer to Sunion Webb's entire satisfaction. Questions of finance, questions of other operatives to be contacted, and particularly, questions concerning the final phase of the operation. With the picture clarified in his mind, Webb twice repeated his instructions. On the second repetition he scarcely paused for a word. He had everything clear in his mind.

Webb left Markov's office at about 10 A.M. Thinking he was to be taken immediately to the main Moscow airport, he was surprised to find his driver choose a route in almost exactly the contrary direction. He asked about it and was told that he would be flown to the main airport from a smaller airstrip. He accepted the information without apprehension, and indeed the information turned out to be precisely correct. The light aircraft which he boarded an hour later took him in a few minutes to the main airport. After landing, it taxied for about half a mile to a point about two hundred yards from a loaded Aeroflot plane. Helping hands lifted Sunion Webb and his bag down onto the apron. Then at a run across the concrete he was shepherded to the waiting plane, so that by the time he had pounded his way up the gangway he was quite out of breath. One of the hostesses took his bag and another conducted him with a smile to his seat.

After takeoff, and before settling down to read, he wondered about the light aircraft. To avoid being seen, perhaps, seen by some CIA agent in the main airport lounge? He was gratified to think that such fine details were being taken care of. This made him wonder about the frankness

with which Igor Markov had described his plan. He was
gratified too that such a deep trust should have been
placed in his integrity.

It never occurred to Sunion Webb that had he de-
murred, had he expressed doubts about any important
aspect of the plan, the car which had driven him to the
airstrip would have driven him to a very different place,
a place where his executioners would have been waiting.

It was just 3 P.M. as Sunion Webb reached the Rozen
Moat in Amsterdam. He crossed the Singel and Da Costa
canals, and then turned left into Bilderdijk Street where
his hotel was located. It was a small hotel taking about
twenty persons. He checked in, signed the register, produced his British passport, and was then shown by a slim
woman of about fifty up to his room. Here he took off
his jacket, rolled up his shirt sleeves, and washed his face.
Then he slumped down suddenly in the only chair.

Sunion Webb had already finished the first of the three
parts of his assignment. The third part was really the
hardest, but he had been much less worried about the
third part than about the first part, because the third
part belonged to his own world, whereas this first part
was clandestine. Actually it had proved very easy. Webb
had left the Aeroflot flight at Schipol Airport, passing
without difficulty through Dutch immigration and customs. It was just 12:15 P.M. when he had hired a taxi
which had taken him from the airport into Amsterdam.
He told the driver to drop him at the main post office,
opposite the Rozen Moat from the Royal Palace. Since
he still had half an hour to spare, he then walked into
the open space of the Dam where he bought a generous-
sized beef sandwich and a cup of coffee.

Half past one o'clock found him back at the Singel
Canal, at a point where the tourist boats put in. His in-

struction had been to take the first open boat, not the usual covered boats, to arrive there after 1:30 P.M. This he had done, seating himself on a vacant wooden bench. Almost immediately a man had pushed in and sat beside him. Sunion Webb remembered the mop of fair hair and the dark glasses. Beyond that he remembered little except that the man had obviously been young and he seemed quite fat. The dark glasses fitted Webb's instructions, and so did the young man's opening remark: "It looks as though the skies will be clouding in." Since the afternoon was already quite grey, with the skies thoroughly overcast, Sunion Webb had been in no doubt that here was his contact. He and the young man had walked over to the boat rail at the rear, where there was a good deal of engine noise. Because of the noise and because the boat was open, there was no danger of their conversation being overheard. Sunion Webb had then put the proposition he had been told to put. He had been told to use French, and this he had also done. The young man had made no response, which had been something of a difficulty, for Sunion Webb was by his nature a propagandist. His instinct had been to persuade. The young man's lack of response had therefore been a disappointment, especially when the fellow had quit the boat about halfway through its circuit of the city. Thereafter, Webb had continued back to the starting point, not far from the post office. Leaving the boat, he had simply walked to the hotel.

As he sat now, he realised that it had certainly not been his job to persuade the young man, and this was something of a relief to him. There was a knock. With a sudden kick of his heels he jumped spryly from his chair to the door, to find the slim proprietress standing there with a tray of tea. Muttering thanks, he accepted the tray. The woman stayed for a minute or two, chatter-

ing away, interrupting his thoughts. He told her that he
had just come in from Paris by the afternoon train. When
she had gone he was angry with himself. Two years ago
he had travelled from Paris to Amsterdam by the afternoon train. But was it running still? He decided he should
have given a better answer.

He poured himself a cup of tea. As he sipped the hot
liquid he wondered about the fair young man. He wondered how the young man had picked him out so unerringly. What would have happened if the open tourist
boat had come along a minute or two earlier before 1:30
P.M. instead of a minute or two afterward? It never occurred to him how infinitely easy it had all been for Igor
Markov. A KGB agent had travelled on the same Aeroflot
plane. After arrival at Schipol, the agent had met up with
the fair young man. Indeed, the fair young man had come
that morning from Frankfurt to Amsterdam in response
to a first contact from another of Markov's operatives.
And the KGB man together with the fair young man
had simply waited there near the post office, waited for
Sunion Webb to return after eating his sandwich.

Libya, Afternoon

The car provided by the Soviet Trade Mission took
the courier Alex Semjanov into the luxurious al-Fuwayhat
suburb of Benghazi. It was a district of expensive villas
made colourful by flower-filled gardens, which owed their
existence to water piped from deep wells sunk in the
desert to the south. Without water all this fragrance
would immediately have lapsed into the desert from
which it had recently sprung. So Semjanov reflected as
he reclined in the rear of the car. All the while he
clutched a briefcase to his side, just as he had done from
the time he had left Moscow. The flight had been a direct

one by Aeroflot, otherwise the briefcase would not have been permitted. It would inevitably have been inter- cepted and opened at one or another of the security checks operated by other international airlines. While its twenty-pound weight was not particularly unusual in itself, the briefcase felt peculiar, because the weight within it was highly concentrated, concentrated almost to a point. It felt as if there were a heavy thing in there surrounded by a lot of lightweight packing material.

The meeting with Colonel Abdul Hassim, representing the Libyan Ministry of Defence, had been set up by the Soviet Trade Mission in Benghazi rather than in Tripoli because it was less likely to be noticed there by the Libyan government's own civil servants who were mainly domi- ciled in Tripoli.

The car swung into an open gate with high white pillars at its sides. Flanking the drive, which was fully two hun- dred yards long, were two rows of dark cypress trees. There was a short flight of wide stone steps leading up to a villa which owed its architectural style to the civilisa- tions of Greece and Rome rather than to its present Is- lamic owners. Scipio Africanus would have been at home there, provided of course that he was unaware of the contents of the briefcase which Alex Semjanov carried up the steps, a briefcase which Semjanov still held to himself with visible care.

A servant in a white robe showed him to a room on the upper level. Colonel Hassim was waiting to greet him. There was no interpreter and, ironically, in view of the purpose of the meeting, the language the two men used was English, the common denominator of human communication—for Hassim had no Russian and Semja- nov had no Arabic. Back in Moscow, Igor Markov had thought of sending an Arabic speaker, but he had eventu- ally decided that the language used was not a primary

consideration. Technical understanding and the understanding of human nature and human weaknesses were
more important factors.

The offer which had been made to Colonel Abdul Hassim seemed almost too good. Too good for what was being
asked in exchange. The latest, most sophisticated strategic
air missiles seemed overwhelmingly more important than
the simple briefcase which Semjanov had carefully placed
upon a table. There was never any doubt in Colonel Hassim's mind that he would accept the Russian offer, for
no briefcase could equal a SAM installation in its importance to his country. But why was the briefcase so important to the Russians? Hassim continued the conversation
for a while in the hope that he might find out, but at
length he concluded that Semjanov simply did not know
himself, and hence further persistence would be useless.
Without further dissembling, he agreed to do what was
required.

Alex Semjanov bowed himself out, leaving Colonel Hassim staring at the briefcase on the table. Semjanov wondered at leaving it behind, but that indeed had been
his instruction.

Colonel Hassim wondered about opening the briefcase,
but then reflected that by doing so he stood to lose the
SAM missiles. Worse, the Russians might make his decep-
tion known to his own government, and with the loss
of the missiles his own power could well be forfeit. Worse
still, the briefcase probably contained a bomb, in which
case both the missiles and his life might be lost. At length
he decided it would be simplest and safest to do with it
precisely what had been asked of him. In arriving at this
decision Hassim had followed the pattern of thought
which had been planned for him in the flow chart of
Igor Markov. For Igor Markov had known that no truly
curious man, no man of the type who would actually

open the briefcase, could have risen to Hassim's position
in the revolutionary government of Libya. Real curiosity
would long ago have brought about its own downfall.

With a sigh of frustration Colonel Hassim picked up
the briefcase, taking it with him down to the car which
would speed him to the Benghazi airport. A gaudily coloured parrot screamed as he climbed into the car, and
he wondered who among his neighbours had been fool
enough to import such an absurd bird.

East Berlin, Afternoon

Captain Luri Otto was not an entirely first-class courier.
Of his loyalty to the Communist cause there was no question; the problem lay with his natural sense of curiosity.
He liked to know what was going on, entirely for his
own satisfaction, of course. In his pilot's duty case there
were now two highly dense, sealed packages, each weighing about ten kilograms. The packages were differently
wrapped, one in bright yellow, the other in a drab dun
colour.

The duty case had been packed for him in Moscow,
before the commencement of his flight to Berlin. At 9:30
A.M., two hours before the scheduled flight time, his case
had been collected from his room at the Leningrad Hotel.
It had subsequently been returned to him. In fact, he
had found it there in the cockpit when he had boarded
his plane. Curiosity had dictated that at some moment
during the flight he should open it up. When he had
done so, he had found the two packages embedded there
among his own articles and materials. Nothing else had
changed.

The sheer density of the packages suggested nuclear
materials to the enquiring mind of Luri Otto. The thought
occurred to him that moving the two pieces toward one

another would surely bring an immediate disaster for himself, his plane, and its hundred and thirty passengers. The thought brought out in him an instant cold sweat, and with a sudden snap he closed the duty case. The sooner he was rid of it, the better. The moment when he would hand it on to his contact suddenly seemed infinitely to be desired. Then as he gradually settled himself into a calmer mood, he remembered an odd circumstance. One of the two packages, the one with the drab dun-coloured wrapping, had been distinctly warm to his touch, but strangely enough the temperature of the yellow wrapped package had seemed quite normal.

Luri Otto was forty-seven years old, his hair and eyes light brown. Just six feet in height, he was not quite as fit as an airline pilot should properly be. Yet his safety record in the air was excellent, although he had been involved some years earlier in a road accident which had left a two-inch scar along the right side of his jawline. His flight had been delayed in Moscow for technical reasons by three hours, which meant that takeoff had not been until about 14.30. Once in the air, the German Democratic Republic plane had encountered no further difficulty. The flight had been smooth in spite of its captain's anxieties, and a landing had been effected at Schönefelt Airport just at 15.57 local time.

The delay in takeoff had infuriated Igor Markov, who was still working at his desk in the Babushkin suburb. A large map with sundry coloured flags stuck in it was now mounted on one of the office walls. Igor Markov had thought about lighting a white-hot fire under the mechanics at Moscow Airport, but he reluctantly decided that any obvious interference with normal civil processes would be noticed and reported in places where he had no wish for it to be reported.

The duty case was now too heavy for it to be a normal

duty case. A close observer might have noticed that Luri
Otto was making an unusual effort to carry it in an apparently normal way as he passed through the standard airport formalities. But the East German officials paid only
cursory attention to passengers and air personnel arriving
from Moscow. And, as a last resort, Luri Otto could have
prevented a search of his case through an appeal to the
airport security chief, who would have laid the red carpet
out for him if need be. But there was no need for emergency measures. Which was good, for a hitch of any kind
in normal procedures is never welcome to the likes of
Luri Otto. Outside the airport entrance he walked toward
a row of taxis, the duty case hanging like a lump of lead
on his arm. He allowed other passengers to take the first
wave of the taxis, waiting himself until one came and
stopped there without bothering to pull in close to the
kerbside. He went across to it and stepped inside. A duty
case exactly like his own was standing upright on the
cab floor. With the assurance that he had indeed chosen
the right taxi, he gave the driver his home address in
the Kopenickerstrasse.

The driver took him via the Muhlenstrasse, where the
afternoon business traffic was now building up, so that
it was the best part of an hour before he reached the
apartment building where he lived with his wife and son.
He quit the taxi, paid off the driver, and went into the
building carrying the other, much lighter case which he
had picked up from the floor of the cab and leaving his
own. His anxieties had quite gone by the time he greeted
his wife at the threshold of their apartment.

The taxi stopped for a second time behind an empty
Skoda car, apparently to take on another passenger. The
driver got out, opened the rear door, and carefully retrieved Luri Otto's heavy case from the passenger seat.
Meanwhile the supposed passenger mounted into the

driver's seat. In a moment the taxi had swept away, and its original driver had unlocked and let himself into the Skoda. Within another moment the Skoda had pulled away from the kerbside and it too was gone.

It took fully twenty-five minutes in the heavy traffic for the Skoda to reach the Ostbahnhof. The car had a special government parking sticker, which permitted the driver to find a stopping place. Here he opened the duty case and proceeded to handle the two heavy packages in turn. The package in the dun-coloured wrapping was quite warm, and this he put into an old briefcase, which was lying there on the rear seat of the car. The briefcase had been well filled with a rubbery kind of material, and with the aid of this material he was able to wedge the heavy package, the one that was warm, into a stable position. It took a little while to effect this operation, and during the manoeuvre it happened that the two heavy packages were brought closely adjacent to each other. Nothing happened, thus confounding the opinion of Luri Otto.

Carefully locking the car, the sometime taxi driver took the old briefcase into the railway station proper. Near the ticket office he found a row of luggage lockers. Number 29 was apparently in use, for it was closed with no key in its lock—and for the good reason that the driver himself had the key. Or, more precisely, the driver had a key with which he proceeded to open up number 29. There was nothing inside it. As if he had just arrived in search of a locker, the driver then put in the briefcase, put in money, shut the locker door, and withdrew the key. Five minutes later he had made his way back to the Skoda and was on the move again.

He drove a complicated in-and-out route, but in a generally northerly direction until he reached the Berliner Ring. Turning west for a while in moderate traffic, by

6:30 P.M. he had reached the road north to Oranienburg
and Neustrelitz, the road that would take him to Stralsund
near the Baltic coast. It was over two hundred kilometres
to the coast, which he aimed to make before dusk. Because of the delay of the flight from Moscow, and because
of the heavy afternoon traffic in Berlin, he was now some
four hours behind schedule. So there was no time to stop
for dinner, which was a pity, since he had also gone without lunch, and by nature the driver was a good solid
eater.

Hunching himself over the wheel, he tried to forget
the pangs in his stomach. He urged the Skoda as fast as
he could through the fields, lakes, and woods of the north
German plain. At Stralsund he turned to the northeast
on the last stage of his journey to the island of Rugen.
It was just about 10 P.M. when he reached the docks at
the ferry port of Sassnitz, and there was just sufficient
light for him to drive along the wharfside until he could
see the outline of the Soviet steamship *Magnetogorsk.*
Unlike most ships plying up and down the Baltic, the
Magnetogorsk was capable of a high turn of speed, a turn
of speed which would have been uneconomic for a Western commercial shipping company, but which could be
important in matters of a quite different kind.

The driver of the Skoda parked a hundred yards away
from the *Magnetogorsk.* He managed to bring the car
into a position facing directly toward the ship. He then
gave three momentary flashes with his headlights, and
settled himself down to wait, with the pangs of hunger
now rumbling audibly in his belly. Mercifully the wait
was not unduly long, for in a few moments a man in
sailor's attire came alongside. It was a little odd to see
a sailor carrying an airline pilot's duty case. The driver
got out of the car, picked up the case he had brought
from Berlin, and checked that it was of identical outward

appearance to the one the man was carrying. The last part of the driver's assignment was simply to hand over the case, and to take the one carried by the sailor in return. He watched the sailor heading back toward the ship and then he returned to the car, his mind now occupied by just one topic—food.

N. Atlantic, Late Evening

Two hundred miles south-southeast of Rockall, two Russian "fishing trawlers," accompanied by an electronics ship, steamed at full speed toward their rendezvous at the Great Blasket Islands off the coast of Kerry. The captain of the electronics ship was in command of the mission, which he believed to be a simple matter of gunrunning for the IRA. The two trawlers had caught few fish, for in their holds lay crates of small arms and ammunition.

However, there had been some emendation of the original plan. There had been a top priority message from Moscow instructing them to await an air drop timed for 10 P.M. With not too much of the twilight left, the sky being overcast, the captain scanned the eastern horizon anxiously. The top priority worried him.

It came at last, a small military plane. It made a tight turn and then came at them again. This time as it went by a small coloured object emerged from the belly of the plane. It fell on a parachute for about two thousand feet and splashed down into the sea some five hundred yards away from the electronics ship. Half an hour later it had been hauled on board.

Another half hour went by as the object was detached from the parachute, taken to the captain's cabin, and unpacked. It turned out to be nothing but a heavy briefcase which had been fastened securely in a nest of buoyant life vests. The captain scratched his head and wondered about the briefcase. Then he decided that it wasn't his place to wonder about such things. So he opened up the safe in which the ship's documents were kept, put the briefcase inside, and readjusted the combination, troubling himself to check the new digits carefully.

Waiting for the air drop had cost almost three hours of time. The captain returned to the bridge. He knew their position within a few miles, but he wanted to make absolutely sure of it. They were pretty well plumb over the centre of the Rockall Deep, which meant that rendez-vous was still another two hundred miles away. At full speed it would be 6 A.M. before they reached Great Blasket, at least two hours later than the captain would have wished.

Hermann Kapp and Others

Darmstadt, Early Morning

Hermann Kapp glanced at his watch. 2:17 A.M. He found
it impossible to sleep. Hermann Kapp was chubby but
not fat. He looked fat to the casual eye, but under the
surface layer of fat he was solidly and powerfully muscled,
as the girl who lay tucked by his side knew full well.
By now Susi had had enough and had fallen soundly
asleep. Her fine blonde hair was strewn across the pillow,
tickling his nose, and helping to keep him awake. Uncon-
sciously she kept close to him, moving whenever he did.
The August night was warm and he thought about pushing her away. But then she would waken as like as not,
with the inevitable consequences, for after learning that
he was going abroad for a while she was in an insatiable
mood.

More of it was the last thing Hermann Kapp felt he
needed just at the moment. His mind was still reeling
from the proposition he had been given. By the little
man with the brushed-back long white hair, on the boat
in Amsterdam. After leaving the boat, he had walked
to the city office of Lufthansa and taken an airline bus

to Schipol, returning to Frankfurt by the 5:45 P.M. Lufthansa flight. At Frankfurt he had hired a small car, using
one of the several driver's licenses in different names
he always carried with him. Hermann Kapp did not own
a car of his own because private cars are easily traced.
He changed the cars he hired frequently, often ringing
the changes on the different licenses. Hermann Kapp
always hired small inconspicuous cars because he liked
to be inconspicuous, at any rate until the big moments
came along.

He thought carefully about the three others he would
choose, assuming the little man's proposition did not turn
out to be a hoax. They would need to be top people
with special skills, all dedicated artists, all with clean
noses. A skilled mechanic, of course, and an explosives
buff. The electronics he would fix himself, naturally. This
left the fourth spot for a bodyguard. His mind turned
naturally to Félix. He had worked with the woman before.
Odd to think of using a woman as a bodyguard, but sex
was no discriminator where quickness was concerned,
and Félix had just about the quickest reactions with a
pistol or rifle of anybody he'd ever seen. She had given
instruction to special IRA squads, which might be a disadvantage for this job, though. Hermann Kapp put the point
aside as he thought for a while about Abu l'Weifa, otherwise known as Pedro-the-Basque. It was a good alias. It
had to be, because to this point it had kept Israeli intelligence off his trail.

His mind jerked back to Félix. Tall with close-cropped
auburn hair, big hands, and the almost breastless, slender
body of a female ballet dancer. Sexless, thought Hermann
Kapp, to men at any rate, but reportedly dominating
and ruthless in her lesbian relations toward soft little
things like Susi. The thought made his penis come up
hard again. He forced his knee between Susi's thighs,

and had her mounted by the time she awoke. As the sensations flooded into her consciousness, she made little gasping cries, as if she felt herself to be at the point of drowning. He didn't think about Susi, or about enjoying himself. It was the thought of the job, the proposition which filled his mind, giving him a sense of overwhelming power. He used his strength on Susi so that some minutes later, when he drew away from the girl, her breath was coming in long shuddering sobs. Without comment, he rolled out of the bed, and went through to the kitchenette where he started a pot of coffee.

Basel, Switzerland, Noon

Hermann Kapp sat in the banker's office, unusually for him without the tinted glasses which he normally wore in public like a badge of his trade. The banker had just told him that a million Swiss francs had indeed been deposited in the numbered account. So the proposition which the little man in Amsterdam had put to him was for real. Nobody, Hermann Kapp thought, wastes a million Swiss francs in a game of bluff.

He had started early that morning from Darmstadt, but he had made no attempt to hurry his journey to Basel. He had crossed the Rhine near Mannheim and had continued south into France. At Strasbourg he had turned in the hired car. From there he had taken a train into Switzerland, leaving it at the Basel station. Hermann Kapp was not a disguise artist. His face was too chubby and his muscular frame too distinctive for any subtle disguise to be possible for him. The tinted glasses were not really for disguise, but so that people couldn't easily guess what he was thinking. In place of disguise Hermann Kapp persistently broke up his movements into pieces which he tried to make as self-contained as possible. He had troubled himself to drive into France to turn in the car because tracing a hired car takes that bit longer when an international frontier has been crossed. Then he had made the train journey to disconnect his movements from the car journey.

He had waited until the train reached the Schweitzer Bahnhof in Basel before getting himself some breakfast, because it was essentially impossible for him to be noticed and remembered there whereas some fellow passenger might conceivably have remembered had he breakfasted on the train. It wasn't that Hermann Kapp was neurotic about his movements, or that he was thinking about them all the time. Such precautions had become as natural to him as breathing.

From the Schweitzer Bahnhof he had followed the tramway along the Elisabethanstrasse until he had reached the bank, the Société des Banques Suisses. He had asked for the director but the director had been busy. He was then introduced to one of the assistant directors. Deciding this was good enough, he had made his inquiry about the million francs. Assured that the million francs was there, Hermann Kapp had then come to the critical point, which was to change the number of the account with the money in it. For Kapp wanted a number known only to himself. The banker asked to see his passport. The passport, being issued by the German Federal Republic, and there being no currency restrictions between West Germany and Switzerland, the banker consequently felt satisfied that his customer was not engaging in any obvious fraud. Nor was there any infringement of Swiss law, which was the banker's real concern. So the matter was quickly settled, and by ten minutes after noon Hermann Kapp left the bank a million francs richer, a million francs now safe from prying eyes, in his own personal account.

The next step was to disconnect himself from the visit to the bank, not because he had grounds for thinking he might be followed, but just as a matter of habit. Outside the bank he hailed a taxi and rode to Basel Airport. It was more or less irrelevant where he went to begin with from there. Seeing a Swissair flight due out almost immediately for Milan, he took it. An hour later he was riding in a bus from Milan Airport into the city. In the city he lunched at a trattoria in a side street. Then he walked to the railway station in ample time to catch the afternoon express for Paris and London. Close by the railway station he found a post office, from which he sent a telegram to an individual known as Louis-le-Poisson in Paris.

Göteborg, Sweden, 7 A.M.

With the exception of the passage through the fifty miles of confined waters between the coasts of Denmark and Sweden, the master of the Soviet steamship *Magnetogorsk* had driven his vessel at full speed all through the night and through the hours after dawn. Indeed, he had received a special signal from Moscow instructing him to reach Göteborg by 7 A.M. Igor Markov's original plan had called for a 5 A.M. arrival, but the delay at Moscow Airport on the previous day had forced the *Magnetogorsk* into a furious midnight dash, with its powerful turbines causing the ship to shudder in its timbers from bow to stern. But arrive in Göteborg they had, by the prescribed 7 A.M. A berthing place had been prearranged. The master drew the *Magnetogorsk* into it just as the Kristine Church clock was chiming the hour.

No sooner were the gangplanks down than port officials followed by stevedores came on board. Once it was seen that the ship's papers were in order, the stevedores busied themselves in preparing to unload a quantity of cargo. Among them was Ole Gröte, a thickset, thick-necked man wearing a black sweater and woolly hat against the cool of the early morning air. One moment he was there with the others, the next moment he was gone unr.oticed, for nobody on the wharfside has much regard for the comings and goings of stevedores. He carried a small but heavy package to a modest-sized warehouse which stood on the waterfront immediately beside a larger warehouse. Taking a key from his pocket, he unlocked a side door to the smaller warehouse, and then made his way with unerring steps to an unlocked office. Another key permitted him to open a cabinet from which he took a number of small lead tags and an embossing machine, used for locking the tags to a length of wire.

Knowing that it was getting dangerously late, Gröte moved quickly out into the yard beside the warehouse, carrying the tags and the embossing machine as well as the heavy package. Letting himself into the larger warehouse, he studied a number of containers. It took a few precious moments to find the right one, a container of Volvo spares addressed to Coventry, England. With wire cutters from his pocket he snipped away the seal and the wire which had been used to complete the fastening of the container. The broken bits he put carefully into a pocket. To open the container he now had only to deal with a large padlock which held the main retaining bolt. The padlock was simple, yielding to a big key on a ring, which hung from one of the warehouse walls. Ole Gröte now pushed the heavy package between two cartons, making sure it was secure there, but otherwise not bothering to conceal it. Quickly he closed up the container, ramming home the bolt and clicking the padlock shut. It remained to seal the bolt in position with a new piece of wire, and an embossed lead tag.

His time had run out. A car could be heard pulling
up in the yard between the two warehouses. Glancing
through the door of the main warehouse, he saw that
the driver of the car had gone into the smaller building.
Gröte did not hesitate. Quickly he moved outside, opened
the driver's door, and sounded the horn long and loud.
Then he ducked out of sight behind a corner of the small
warehouse. A moment later the owner of the car came
out to see what was going on. He opened the door and
was peering down into the interior as Ole Gröte struck
him a heavy blow with the embossing machine. The fellow made a faint, pathetic whispering sound, really an
exhalation of breath, as he went down.

Inside the smaller warehouse, in the office once more,
Ole Gröte replaced the embossing machine and the spare
lead tags. He did not bother to relock the cabinet. Instead
he simply took from it a metal cash box, which he carried
under one arm, hidden inside his jersey. Two hundred
yards further along the wharf, as he walked alongside a
large vessel, he jettisoned the cash box into the sea. He
watched the box go down through the narrow gap between the ship and the dockside, down into deep water.
His job was done, but the late arrival of the *Magnetogorsk*
had surely run it fine for him.

An hour later, containers destined for Humberside,
England, were in the process of being loaded into a cargo
vessel. Three of the containers carrying Volvo spares had
been delayed for upwards of an hour by the police. The
police had arrived about 8:15 A.M., following the discovery of a seriously injured man lying inert beside the warehouse where the Volvo containers had been stored. The
injured man had been taken away to the hospital, and
the police had then questioned the warehouse staff. It
had soon been determined that a cash box containing
upwards of five thousand kroner was missing from a

nearby office. Convinced that robbery was the cause of the assault, the police had inspected the large warehouse only in a cursory manner, and had then seen no reason to interfere any longer with the containers being loaded aboard the ship. The journey to England would take about a day and a half, and in that time many other details of the plan of Igor Markov would have time to develop.

Berlin, East Germany, Morning

It was the courier Klaus Hartstein's first assignment in more than a year. As he'd shaved that morning in the apartment that was rented for him close by the Chauseestrasse, within a short distance of the Wall, he had tried to persuade himself that he was glad to be back. He was a heavy man of middle height and late middle age, with a developing Mr. Pickwick kind of appearance. The previous evening he had examined the papers he had been given. He was to travel ostensibly on behalf of the Fritz Weiss Optical Company of Jena, and there was a file of letters from Weiss to customers in West Germany, France, and England which he could offer to prove it. His passport had the right name and photograph on it, but it had visas and immigration stampings relating to past journeys which Klaus Hartstein had never made himself. In addition to these papers and documents there was a generous issue of foreign currency, and Hartstein was certainly glad of this.

From his apartment he had walked to the small garage where the Volkswagen was kept. Even at the early hour of 6 A.M. a mechanic had been there to tell him about it. Then he had driven to the Ostbahnhof where he had retrieved an old, rather battered briefcase from locker 29, close by the ticket office. With the briefcase safely on the back seat of the car he had driven a little way

southeast to pick up the outer ring road which avoids
West Berlin. He had followed the ring road to the Leipzig
exit. From Leipzig, where he had breakfasted at about
9 A.M., he had continued southwest toward Jena. He had
not troubled to go into the town itself, however, but had
bypassed both Jena and Weimar to the south. Travelling
directly west now, the road had risen into the Thuringen-
wald, with its extensive forests of dark spruce. After con-
sulting a large scale map of the Eisenach district, he had
located a small side road which brought him to the place
the mechanic in Berlin had told him about. It was a se-
cluded spot in the forest, appropriate for the job he now
had to do. He knew it was the right spot because there
was a small hut with two cans of petrol inside it, and
there was a pipe with a stream of water coming out of
it at shoulder height above the ground.

Klaus Hartstein had himself received some training as
a mechanic. So he had little doubt of his ability to perform
the job which lay ahead. First he stripped right down
to his underclothes. Then he opened up the front of the
VW and took out a set of spanners. The ones he would
need for the job had been specially marked, and with
these he took off the fuel tank from the bottom of the
car. This proved less difficult than he feared because
someone had recently made sure that none of the fittings
were rusted in. He then emptied the tank, letting the
petrol flow away in the stream of water. Turning the
tank upside down on the grass, he scraped away the accu-
mulated dust and dirt from an area about a finger span
across. Inlaid there in a thin layer of wax were four flat-
ended screws. These he quickly removed, and out came
a plate to reveal a shallow compartment lying between
the false bottom and the true bottom of the tank. Into
this compartment he put the dun-wrapped package contained in the old briefcase which he had retrieved from

locker 29 at the Ostbahnhof. His senses being thoroughly acute, he noticed the package to be distinctly warm, and this set him to wondering what it might be. After contemplating this problem for a moment or two, he replaced the plate and then tightened the four flat-ended screws into their bedding in the false bottom of the tank. Around each one of them he now squeezed a liquid wax that would soon set firm. The wax would prevent the screws from becoming loose due to the vibrations of the car. He levelled the whole plate with a new coat of the sticky liquid, and then before it dried he smeared a handful of mud from the stream underneath the whole bottom of the tank.

It took a while to replace the fuel tank to his satisfaction because, as well as making sure that all the brackets and bolts were secure, he had to dirty them up, which he did with more of the mud from the stream, making sure that it stuck by first giving the metal a coating of the wax liquid. Then he collected the empty briefcase and all the tools and took them to the little hut, from which he returned with the petrol cans. Next he poured in a little petrol, just to check that the tank had not sprung a leak. Thankful that it had not, he poured in the full contents of both cans. The empty cans he immediately returned to the hut. The last step of all now was to clean himself off at the water pipe. He used a tin of soft soap for this, drying himself with his underclothes. Putting on new underclothes from his travelling bag, and donning his suit again, his last gesture was to throw the tin of soap and the old underclothes into the hut before locking the door. Moments later he was out on the main road, on his way to Eisenach and thence to the West German frontier. The work had made him warm, and his cherubic face had a glow about it as he drove along.

Great Blasket, Morning

The captain of the electronics ship was much worried
by the lateness of the hour. His idea had been to make
landfall just at dawn and to have completed the transfer
of his cargo well before 6 A.M., by which time the farmers
two or three miles away on the Kerry mainland would
be stirring in their beds. It was now two hours later than
this and the operation would be exposed in full view,
not just of a chance individual, but of the whole Dunquin
area.

The captain had telegraphed his apprehensions back
to Moscow, but remarkably enough he had been ordered
to go right ahead regardless. Consequently, the two trawlers and the electronics vessel stood off the island and
boats were launched to carry the material ashore. Consol-
ing himself with the thought that the operation was no
longer his responsibility, the captain put his best efforts
into making sure that it was all done and completed by
midmorning. He went across to Great Blasket himself,
checking the crates, making sure that photographs of
their positioning were properly taken. With him when
he went ashore was the briefcase which had been
dropped so mysteriously from the skies on the previous
evening. The captain was among the last to leave the
island. Before doing so, he made sure the briefcase was
left among the ruins of the old village, just as his extensive
instructions required him to do.

Moscow, 8 A.M.

Igor Markov had drawn a deep sigh of relief the moment news from Sweden informed him of the completion
of the transfer of the yellow-wrapped package from the
Magnetogorsk to the container of Volvo spares. He knew

he really should have cancelled this component of the operation, because of the inadvertent delay of Luri Otto's plane. But this particular manoeuvre was in some respects the *pièce de résistance* of his whole plan, and being proud of it, he had allowed the move to be made, successfully as it had fortunately turned out. As insurance, however, he had activated an alternative plan as early as 1 P.M. on the previous day. As there was no need now for the alternative plan, orders for it to be abandoned would be transmitted immediately from Markov's offices.

An elderly female messenger knocked at his door, and then came in immediately with a single sealed envelope. She did so without bothering to wait for his shout and without any expression crossing her stolid face. When the woman had gone, Igor Markov took the envelope to a corner of the office where there was a device rather like a small reading lamp. He put the envelope, address downward, below the lamp and flicked a switch. Nothing from the lamp itself could be seen to the eye, but an unbroken fluorescence appeared along the sealing of the envelope. Flicking off the switch, and returning to his desk, he now slit open the envelope. Inside was his permission to use Soviet Embassy officials abroad, but subject to severe restraints. Only trade officials, not diplomats, were allowed, and even then for communications purposes only. And after completion of any assignment the officials in question were to be withdrawn immediately.

In case of accident, the permission might well be important, so Igor Markov immediately filed it himself to make absolutely certain he had it safe. As he returned to his desk the memory of a signal from the gunrunning ships into Eire ran momentarily through his mind. Igor Markov could understand the captain's concern at the apparent lateness of the landing on the offshore island with the curious name; Great Blasket, wasn't it? But there had been nothing wrong in the timing of that little incident. Igor Markov permitted himself a flicker of a smile as he reflected on how very little each individual understood of the structure of an operation as vast as this one would turn out to be.

London, Noon

Dr. Ernest Carruthers was a convinced Marxist of a gentle, obstinate type, of which many examples are to be found in the universities. Most of his colleagues at Imperial College thought he had a one-track mind on the subject and they had learned to avoid argument with him, on politics at least. Argument with him was an unrewarding experience, to say the least, for he would always return in his quiet, unassuming voice to precisely the position from which he started. He was frequently to be found at meetings of the Anglo-Soviet Peace Association and he was an ardent attender at the international meetings of PUGWASH. He was also to be found at social occasions organized by the Soviet Embassy, when his thin, very tall figure and his convinced manner would always attract an island of people around him.

He was a frequent visitor to the Soviet Union itself, and was indeed a corresponding member of the Academy of Sciences of the USSR. His technical speciality lay in the field of the chemistry of petroleum products, in which subject he was a Reader at the University of London. At the age of fifty, he had been a candidate for fellowship of the Royal Society. His friends claimed he had been "done down" in the Royal Society elections because of his Marxist views, while those who were less friendly said that his subject was a little too much on the technological side. The matter had left more of a scar than he cared to admit.

It was two minutes after 11:30 as he emerged from the Soviet Embassy in Kensington Palace Gardens. He had gone there in connexion with his next visit to Moscow. The embassy had telephoned to ask that his visit be advanced in time, because otherwise his friends in Moscow would be out of the city. So he had gone along to the embassy to receive his visa, to find that indeed the officials there wanted him to travel already on the 13th. In his patient, obstinate way he had explained several times to the officials that his commitments would not permit him to leave as early as the 13th, but that he thought he might make arrangements for the 16th. Ernest Carruthers thought, if there was just one thing he had against the Russians, it was their lack of a proper sense of time.

Over the years, in fact several times during the previous five years, Ernest Carruthers had helped the Anglo-Soviet Peace Association by bringing small pieces of property to the society's notice, property which could be used to provide accommodations for visitors from the Soviet Union, especially at times like August when the ordinary hotels were overflowing with tourists. With his retentive memory, Carruthers might have remembered 17A Courtlane Mews. Which was precisely why it would have been an advantage to Igor Markov to have him out of the country by the 13th of the month, at the latest.

Dublin, 3:15 P.M.

Father O'Donovan had celebrated his seventieth birthday two and a half weeks ago. Although he was not thin, he looked frail, and in a medical sense he was far from well, as the blue tinge of his lips showed only too ominously. His forward stoop made him look smaller than his real height of five feet nine. Although at one time

his eyesight had been excellent, he had worn glasses for
the past twenty years to correct a developing astig-
matism.

The man who showed him the book was twenty-five
years younger, spare but vigorous, and of some consequence in patriotic circles. He had explained to Father
O'Donovan what had to be done, and it was simple
enough in God's conscience, just to take this bit of a briefcase through customs at the Rosslare-to-Fishguard crossing. It was a comfort to Father O'Donovan to feel that
even at his age, and in his condition, he could still be
of a little consequence to the lads. He had seen much
injustice in his time, especially in the years following the
First World War, which was not so far away after all.

Father O'Donovan was more concerned about the
manner of it than he was about the nature of his task.
For somebody had cut away the inside of a Bible to make
a place for the thing he was to carry, and Father O'Donovan severely disapproved of this despoiling of the holy
book. He had said so, and he hoped the misguided lad
who had done the thing would be seeking dispensation
from his priest.

London, 3:30 P.M.

Sunion Webb walked a short distance along Kensington
Gore before turning left into Queen's Gate. He was carrying a briefcase and, in spite of its weight, there was something of a lilt in his step. He had taken the midmorning
KLM flight from Amsterdam to Heathrow. It had occurred to him as he had passed through immigration that
his arrival in the United Kingdom would probably be
noted. It would be known that he was in the country,
but apart from noting this fact, it was unlikely there would
be any attempt to keep him under close surveillance.

With all its many troubles, the weak British government had plenty of other things to worry itself about. So he had taken a taxi from the airport to the Cumberland Hotel, near Marble Arch. He had checked into a room, had lunched there, and had then taken another cab, this time to an exhibition at Burlington House, immediately off Piccadilly. After paying the cabby, instead of bothering with the exhibition he had walked to Piccadilly Circus and had taken the underground to Knightsbridge. From there it was a short walk to the Libyan Embassy in Prince's Gate. After showing his passport, he had been given the briefcase which he was now carrying.

His walk took him down Queen's Gate to Cromwell Road. Crossing to the south side, he continued west along Cromwell Road, watching the street names to his left until he reached Ashburn. Turning left there, in another hundred yards or so he came to Courtlane Road, and in a further five minutes he arrived at 17A Courtlane Mews. He rang the bell and waited.

Igor Markov had told him of 17A Courtlane Mews and a little of its history. For some years it had been under the apparent auspices of the Anglo-Soviet Peace Association. City rates were paid regularly by the association, and the property was looked after by an elderly couple. Since the place had never yet been "used," it could be considered entirely safe. It was also equipped, so Igor Markov had said.

A grey-haired man in his shirt sleeves half-opened the door, and then opened it more fully. Sunion Webb was slightly surprised to find that his arrival had apparently been expected. He went in, passing a remark on the weather. The grey-haired man had clearly been instructed to show him over the place. Omitting the quarters occupied by the couple, it had three bedrooms each with single beds, a moderate-sized lounge, and a base-

ment. The basement was the *pièce de résistance* of the
place. It had been fitted up as a workshop with a lathe
and sundry other machine tools and with a considerable
quantity of electrical circuitry, components, and hand
tools. The grey-haired man left him to survey the workshop. A safe was set into one of the walls, and Sunion
Webb found that sure enough it could be opened by the
combination he had been given. He placed the briefcase
inside the safe and then reset the dials.

A rather ample woman of about sixty-five appeared
when he went upstairs again. In London speech border-
ing on cockney she invited him to a cup of tea. The cup
of tea turned out to be a full-fledged afternoon tea, which
Sunion Webb took pleasurably in the couple's comfortably furnished sitting room. The woman was a more avid
conversationalist than her husband, and she had a com-
mendably light hand with the scones and cakes she had
baked. The husband came in and sat down to tea, switch-
ing on television to watch cricket as he settled himself
comfortably in an armchair.

Sunion Webb walked back to Knightsbridge station,
reflecting with satisfaction that the "safe" house could
scarcely be any safer. Once more he took the underground, this time to Marble Arch. Back at the Cumberland he returned to his room, took a bath, changed his
clothes, and set himself to face the most tedious part of
his assignment. To wait there until the fair young man
from the boat in Amsterdam should contact him, if indeed
the fellow had accepted the proposition which had been
put to him.

Chequers, 4 P.M.

With a smile, the Prime Minister poured tea into two
cups, one for himself and one for the Chancellor. He

had enjoyed the round of clock golf they had just played together.

The Chancellor wondered as he sipped tea and gazed across a smooth, well-cared-for lawn toward a colourful flowerbed just what manner of man the Prime Minister could be. He was quite evidently not dismayed in the least by the South African news, not by world opinion, not even by the gunning down in South Africa of representatives of the world's press. He was not dismayed by the retreat in the American position, by a cooling from the position which the United States had been urging only a few days before. Consistency was not an American trait, the Prime Minister had said with a smile, as he had tapped a ball unerringly to sink a two-yard putt. Otherwise the United States would never have become so great a power in the world, he had added.

The Chancellor wondered, in his bull-in-a-china-shop way, if the Americans would really stop the deal. Not at all, the Prime Minister had assured him. The *quid pro quo* would still be offered but much more quietly. The Prime Minister's voice was always very gentle, but he had a well-judged habit of adding curses every now and then, which gave a curious compulsive quality to his remarks. He had told the Chancellor that he himself had no intention of giving way to any kind of sodding Soviet blackmail.

Hook of Holland, 5 P.M.

It had been a long day for Klaus Hartstein. Once across into West Germany he had driven through Kassel and Paderborn to Münster. From Münster he had turned slightly south to Wesel, and thence northwest again to the Dutch border near Arnhem.

At the customs post he had run into a traffic buildup

which had cost him an hour's delay. This had brought
on a fit of nerves, the trouble he'd suffered from a year
back. It was depressing to find the weakness still there.
By the time he reached the passport check he was sweating badly. His present fit of nerves contrasted sharply
with the cool command he'd shown earlier in the day.
The Dutch immigration officer had said it was hot, which
was true, and he had even found it difficult to reply calmly
to this simple remark. Then the officer had asked where
he was going. When he had said London the fellow had
smiled. Klaus Hartstein had remembered the smile all
the way across Holland, wondering if there had been
anything behind it.

And indeed the immigration officer himself had wondered about the sweating Pickwickian figure standing
before him. He had kept wondering through his hours
of duty, and eventually in a free moment he had put
an end to his worrying, by making a report to his superior.
The immigration officer had the feeling that he knew a
drug smuggler when he saw one.

Fishguard, 7:30 P.M.

Father O'Donovan had no worry at all as he came up
to the British customs official at the Rosslare-to-Fishguard
crossing. There was no indication of any guilt in his posture, for the good reason that he didn't feel guilty. He
opened up his briefcase without any foreboding when
the official asked him to do so. The man ran his fingers
quickly and expertly through the newspaper, magazines,
loose sheets of paper, and the Holy Bible, which he had
inside it.

"A bit hot, isn't it?" the man asked.

Father O'Donovan smiled unconcernedly and agreed
that it was a bit hot, for indeed the air in the customs
shed was distinctly warm.

"I wonder if you would mind coming this way, Father?" the man went on.

To the priest's surprise he was led away, and a second customs official immediately took the place of the first one, almost as if they had been waiting for him. But that was impossible, surely? Yet in the room to which he was taken there was a third man, very obviously a policeman. With a slight twitch of his shoulder the policeman came quickly toward him. But to Father O'Donovan, the man never reached him, for suddenly and unaccountedly everything became black and forgotten.

St. John's Wood, 7:50 P.M.

Chief Superintendent Willy Best of the Special Branch had just been to the toilet, and he came bounding up a flight of stairs back to his office as he heard the phone ringing. Willy Best was just about six feet, spare but with plenty of muscle, and still a "goer" in spite of his fifty-five years. His fair hair was receding now, both on top and at the temples. He had a big, well-shaped nose, his eyes were light blue, still with a twinkle in them even after more than thirty years in the force. "Cluny Robertson," he said to himself as he picked up the receiver. It was a trick he always played with himself, guessing who it might be at the other end of the line. This time he was right, as he was about half the time. What he didn't expect was Cluny's news.

"The bugger's dead," said a Scottish voice, far off. Willy Best slumped in his chair. "Dead?" he repeated like a parrot.

"Aye, he just keeled over the moment we pulled him in."

"What sort of fellow was he?"

"Dressed like a priest."

"For god's sake, Cluny, I know that."

"Yes, but he looks like a real priest. Old and frail. Looks as though he was on the verge of heart failure anyway."

Willy Best breathed hard into the mouthpiece of the phone.

"Ye got the havers, man?" asked the distant voice.

"Go on."

"We've got a full circus going down here. Local police, ambulances, customs, shouting Irishmen, the lot."

"Well, make sure you've got the lot. I mean, everything he was carrying, everything in his pockets."

"The Church won't like that."

"I'll bet the Church won't like it. But get everything, beads and all, just the same."

"Will do," came Cluny's reply, in what seemed to Willy Best to be an irreverently cheerful voice.

Cluny Robertson had been a soldier, an officer of the Black Watch. He had elected to retire out of the armed services at the age of thirty, and had then spent three months making up his mind between joining the London police and buying salmon rights to a portion of the coast of the Island of Mull. He had joined the police because he hated London, and so he could always look forward to an eventual retirement in the Highlands. If he had gone to Mull, and if after a year or two he had become dissatisfied with that way of life, why then he would have had nothing at all to look forward to.

Father O'Donovan had been picked up, not because of his briefcase, not because the police had cause to suspect him, but because of a tip-off. There were real tip-offs and false tip-offs, and Willy Best thought he had become fairly expert at telling the difference. From the beginning, though, this particular tip-off had a queer smell about it. To start with, there was no Father O'Donovan on the police lists. Yet there was a real Father O'Donovan they had discovered. So why was the IRA using a onetime agent? Why indeed. Now Willy Best knew the answer. To give the poor old fellow heart failure. So that a hell of a row could be made out of it. To make it easier then for the real agents, especially if they happened also to be priests.

4   *August 14th*

The Terrorists Assemble

Immingham Docks, Humberside, 3 A.M.

Two hours before dawn Ron Weld drove his old Morris
car as close as he dared to the customs area. He was a
slight, wiry young man who had worked all his life at
Immingham. He was widely known there as a dockhand
agitator, an activity which roused his passions far more
than this early morning clandestine stuff. But then he
knew who were his friends and who were not. He knew
who could orchestrate the boys in Newcastle, Glasgow,
Liverpool, and London, to help when he himself had
something boiling on the hob. He knew that one good
turn deserves another, and besides the job wasn't difficult.
It was just that he disliked leaving his girl friend at that
hour in the morning, because, like himself, she was dedicated.

Ron Weld slipped out of the car, closing the door as
quietly as he could. He stood there for two minutes, timing it on his watch, to make sure that nobody was around.
Satisfied, he took out a small leather tool bag from the
boot of the car and then made his way to the perimeter
of the container area. He knew every foot of the place,

exactly where he could climb up the wire, snip away
the barbs at the top, and climb to the other side. The
lighting was stronger than Ron Weld would have liked,
so once again he stood silently for a minute or two, to
make sure he was not being watched. Reassured, he
moved silently through the containers until he found the
ones he wanted, three containers with Volvo spares. The
thing he was looking for was in one of them, and the
nuisance was he didn't know which. Even so, it took only
a few minutes to cut all the seals and unlock the padlocks
with his giggler. He opened all three containers before
he started to search about inside them. He found the
thing inside the second one, a package with a bright yellow wrapping. Since there was no way he could reseal
the containers properly, he contented himself with shut-
ting them, pushing home the bolts, and snapping the
padlocks. It made no difference to him what the customs
bastards thought about it, or the shipping bastards, or
any other kind of bastard. He put the yellow-covered
thing, damned heavy for so small an object, into his
leather bag. The climb out over the fence was more awkward because of the extra weight, but within ten minutes
he was back at his car. As he slipped into the driver's
seat he glanced at his watch. The job had taken only
thirty-five minutes. It was just a matter now of handing
the thing over to the comrade who had asked him to
do the job. After that, he would be back to bed for a
couple of hours, and heigh-ho. Some envious buggers
called him a randy little twerp, but why should he care?

Harwich, 5 A.M.

Klaus Hartstein had spent the summer night on the boat
from the Hook of Holland just sitting wide-awake in the
saloon bar. He had drunk several cups of coffee but no

alcohol. He had kept himself determinedly away from
alcohol, without realising that in doing so he was drawing
attention to himself, for abstention did not match his
cherubic countenance.

Deep within himself Klaus Hartstein was afraid. Like
a hunted animal with keen senses, he knew that in some
way he had aroused the suspicions of the immigration
man back at the Dutch frontier. His skin prickled inces-
santly, and continually in his mind's eye he could see
the flat, strangely warm object he had put into the false
bottom of the petrol tank of the VW. From time to time
he even thought the heat of the object might cause the
petrol to explode, destroying the car, and saving him in
a curious kind of way.

As the boat approached the English coast he wrenched
himself out of the saloon bar, forcing his muscles into
unwilling action. Out on the open deck in the light of
a grey cloudy morning he gazed across the water at the
distant shore. England, the place where from the age
of eighteen to twenty he had spent two wretched years
as a prisoner of war. Perhaps it was the memory of those
two years that was upsetting him now?

A voice came over the loudspeakers asking passengers
to return to their cars. Klaus Hartstein stumbled to a
steep flight of steps which led to the bottom of the ship,
to the car deck. It was all he could manage to do to
climb down safely, for his knees and legs seemed unwilling to support the weight of his ample body. He came
at last to his car and began to search his pockets for the
keys. Nowhere, absolutely nowhere, were they to be
found. A sailor came up to him to ask what the matter
was. In his imperfect but tolerably fluent English he explained about the keys. The man looked inside the car
and then laughed, for the keys were still there in the

ignition switch. Hurriedly he got into the car, trembling uncontrollably.

Engines started around him, and up in front the vehicles began to move. Klaus Hartstein pulled himself together and started up his own car. The noise helped a bit to shield him from his surroundings, but always at the back of his mind was a dark fear of the object which lay concealed at the bottom of his car. So far he had put the thought of what it might be out of his mind, but now he was suddenly powerless to prevent his imagination from assuming full command of his whole being. His mouth was as dry as sand, with a bitter taste to it from all the coffee.

Slowly he eased the car forward. All the muscles of his lower body ached from the long punishing journey of yesterday. At last he came to a high circular ramp which led to the customs hall. A man in grey directed him to one of the customs men. When he was asked if he had anything to declare he shook his head with rather too much emphasis. Then the official told him to open up the car boot, but this he affected not to understand, so the official repeated his request in German and Klaus Hartstein opened up the front of the VW. Lucky the tools and the other things had all been left behind, back in the hut in the woods near Eisenach. The customs man searched about for a while and then said, in German again, that he wished to look inside the car itself. The search was now ominously thorough, far too thorough for a routine examination. The man was plainly looking for something.

At length he desisted and went away into an office. Klaus Hartstein had the idea he was making a telephone call. Then the fellow came out with a metal tape rule and a sheet of paper. He began measuring the car, and when he was done with that he compared his readings with figures on the paper. And at last he did what Hartstein had feared he would do all along. From an inner pocket he took out a sketch of the underneath of the VW and began systematically to compare the car and sketch. Another man came up with a container and a pump, to which was fastened a length of plastic hose.

As the second man took off the filler cap, Hartstein permitted himself the first shaft of hope. He knew exactly what the customs men were going to do, and it wasn't the right idea. They were going to suck out the contents of the fuel tank into the container which they would proceed to fill up to a prescribed mark with more petrol. Then they would pour the whole contents of the container back into the tank, which must not overflow. The idea was to check that no object was concealed in it, thereby reducing its volume. One part of the operation had to be done properly. Klaus Hartstein watched the customs men until he was satisfied that no important quantity of fuel had in fact been left in the tank. Then he turned away and left them to it, for of course they would get the right answer, because the tank had been carefully made to give the right answer. It was a precision-made job, not the work of a bungling amateur.

A policeman appeared with a dog. Klaus Hartstein's pulses kicked at the sight of the policeman, but the dog put him in better spirits again. For now he understood. They thought he was smuggling drugs, and the dog was another wrong idea. His legs still felt weak, but he was relaxing and the sweating under his shirt had stopped. He even managed a smile as he watched the dog sniffing the car inside and out. The men pushed the dog into the car for a second time and once again it sniffed in an aimless and disinterested way. After this second fruitless performance the policeman withdrew the dog, and with a remark which Klaus Hartstein didn't understand, he walked away. The customs men had crestfallen looks about them, and the first one at last brought himself to say he was sorry, although he looked more angry than sorry, as indeed he was. Angry with a tip-off that didn't make sense.

Klaus Hartstein forced himself not to be too quick over repacking the articles which had been taken out of the car and out of the boot. He thought about asking the customs men to do the repacking for him, but recollecting the old saying that pride goes before the fall, he meekly did the work himself. Then moving himself heavily into the driver's seat, he started the engine and drove slowly out of the customs hall.

It was nearly 7 A.M. by the time he reached the end of his mission, the car park at Colchester Railway Station. The yard was nearly empty at this hour, so he had no difficulty at all in choosing a spot about fifty yards from the main exit, within sight of the exit, but not too obviously close to it. He locked the car and the boot, and then walked into the station itself. Glancing at a notice board he saw that a train to Frinton-on-Sea was due out just before eight, and suddenly he had a fancy to go there. He had a fair amount of English money in his pocket, enough for a week or two, and his fancy was to live in comfort for a while in the country in which so long ago he had spent two such miserable years. He booked himself a first-class ticket to this Frinton-on-Sea and then sought out the station buffet, for now he was hungry. It was only a cafeteria stocked with indifferent food, but Klaus Hartstein piled up a tray, and ate at speed with no complaints. A few minutes before eight he left the cafeteria and walked onto the platform, where he summoned confidence enough to ask a porter for the Frinton train. He even bought himself a newspaper before climbing ponderously aboard. The first-class carriages, of the old-fashioned type, were comfortable and Hartstein sank into an ample well-sprung seat. As the train moved out of Colchester into the surrounding countryside, he permitted himself the thought that his nerve had returned. He had succeeded. Naturally it did not occur to him that it had never been intended he should succeed.

Paris, 7:30 A.M.

Louis-le-Poisson did not believe in hiding his light under a bushel. He harangued the proprietor of the small café where he habitually took his breakfast in a loud croaking voice, never hesitating to complain if the coffee or the croissants were not to his liking. He always wore a beret and a fish porter's apron. Many years earlier he had actually worked as a fish porter, and now he owned a small fish business located in a cul-de-sac off the Rue du Sentier. Just so that no inquisitive busybody could fault his knowledge of his stated trade.

Louis-le-Poisson also ran a second business, aristocratic in its style, in total contrast to the plebeian quality of his fish business. Louis ran an agency, and just as high-grade literary or musical agencies restrict the numbers of their clients, so did Louis-le-Poisson restrict his clients, to less than two score of them.

Hermann Kapp was one of Louis' clients. It was to Louis that in Milan on the previous day Hermann Kapp had sent a telegram. Having travelled from Milan to Paris by train, he had met up with Louis, and all through the night Louis had been actively engaged in his particular business. The two of them now sat together in the café. Louis suddenly cried out at the proprietor in a patois which Hermann Kapp did not remotely understand, but from the proprietor's reaction he saw it must simply be a request for more coffee. So he himself nodded at the proprietor and pointed toward his own large bowl of a cup.

Louis-le-Poisson served as an information bureau to his clients. You did not trouble to inform all your acquaintances of your whereabouts; you informed Louis, and Louis could be relied on to pass the information to your friends—provided they had need of it, and provided of course that they really were your friends. Louis had started in the clandestine information business long ago, during the war, when he had served as a radiotelegraph operator for the maquis. Those were the days when radio equipment was bulky and heavy, when it was quite a bother getting it from one place to another. Now it was all so easy that a child could manage these modern fool-proof devices. Louis-le-Poisson was also a mine of information on modes of travel, on the best way for you to get from one place to another, in case you didn't know for yourself. And he watched carefully for the police, not for himself, but for you. He kept files on all the others too, and he could warn you about anybody in a hot situation, so that you didn't get yourself into unwise involvements.

Louis-le-Poisson drank his second bowl of coffee. He had disapproved of Félix, not quite right for this boy Hermann. A good boy, a doctor of electronics from München, the Technische Hochschule there, with plenty of ideas for putting his knowledge to use, instead of becoming a lecturer in some dry-as-dust German collegium. Anna Morgue, alias Félix, was known to Interpol, he had said. She would be looked for at the airports. But the boy would have none of it. He had wanted this Félix, so there had been nothing for it but to locate her, and a devil of a job that had been. It had taken much of the night, and much good might she do him, this man-

bitch whom Louis-le-Poisson did not like. God in hell,
no.

Hermann Kapp knew a few things about Louis-le-Poisson, of which Louis himself was ignorant. The services
which Louis offered at a price to his clients were fine,
so long as Louis' organisation remained unpenetrated.
Far fewer messages were sent flying around that way
than there would have been if everybody communicated
with everybody else all the time, and so there was a
smaller chance that way of the police and of security
agencies happening to hear of something important. But
police penetration of Louis' organisation would instantly
explode the thing sky-high. And because Louis might well
play along with the police in such a situation, not troubling himself to warn his clients, that is to say, it had
been thought expedient to have Louis watched. Louis
didn't know about this, because he was a communications
man, not a watching man. But Hermann Kapp knew
about it. He hoped for Louis' sake that his garden was
still in bloom.

London, King's Cross, 9:30 A.M.

An elderly, rather frail man, the caretaker from Courtlane Mews, watched as the passengers on the express
with sections from Leeds, York, and Hull, came in small
groups through the arrival gate. Suddenly he stepped
forward to greet one of the passengers, a man in a trilby
hat carrying a small but heavy case, a case which he had
received from Ron Weld. The man in the trilby had a
ginger moustache, and he grinned immediately in recognition of the elderly man. The two of them took a taxi
to Marble Arch. When they emerged from the taxi, the
elderly man was holding the case. As soon as the fellow

in the trilby had paid off the cabby, the two separated, the passenger from the north walking briskly east along Oxford Street, and the elderly man, still carrying the case, making his way into a nearby underground station. Half an hour later the elderly man, still carrying the case, emerged from the Gloucester Road station. And a few minutes later still, the same elderly man arrived at 17A Courtlane Mews. His wife opened the door at his ring. It was now only the work of a few seconds to take the case down to the basement and to leave it there.

Neither objects nor walls can speak, but if they could, the object inside the case might have told of its own singular nature, and of its curious experiences since Captain Luri Otto had brought it to East Berlin. And a similarly yellow-wrapped object, lying inside the safe on the wall, might have responded with an almost equally curious account of its own journey from Moscow to 17A Courtlane Mews.

London, St. John's Wood, 9:30 A.M.

"Well, would you have believed it?" asked Willy Best in his cheerful tenor voice.

"Not this side of the Persian Gulf," Cluny Robertson replied without any trace of a smile.

Willy Best could never make up his mind about Cluny Robertson. Did the man have no sense of humour, or was his sense of humour exceedingly subtle? Sometimes Willy Best thought one way about it, sometimes the other. Now he was inclined to think Cluny subtle and deep. Persian Gulf indeed.

There was a heavy knock on the office door, and the Commissioner came straight in.

"Bloody awful business, Best," he began.

"What, the priest?" Willy asked.

"Of course, what else? Seems they're up to some new trick."

"A new trick all right, Sir Stanley."

Cluny Robertson pointed to a table. Without a word, Sir Stanley Farrar, a big six-foot-six man who was heavy without being fat, walked to the table and examined the briefcase carefully, the cutaway Bible, and what seemed to be simply a flat lump of lead.

"What the devil is this? It's hot," he said at length, holding up the lump of lead.

"What would the priest be doing with it?" grunted Cluny Robertson.

"Bringing it into the country, apparently," Willy Best informed the Commissioner.

Willy Best came round from his desk chair to take the leadlike object in his hand.

"I think only the outside of it is lead, Sir. It's too heavy for it all to be lead."

"Something inside?"

"I think so. That's where the heat must be coming from."

"Any ideas?"

"I thought at first it might be some kind of chemical. Chemicals when they're brought together can give quite a lot of heat, but not as much as this."

"It's hot, but not too hot," the Commissioner remarked.

"Yes, but it's been hot for many hours on end. It has to be something which produces heat steadily at a moderate rate, but for a very long time."

The Commissioner thought a moment.

"I see what you mean, Best," he said in a slow, troubled way.

"Aye, it's radioactivity we mean," cut in Cluny Robertson in a brisk voice which convinced Willy Best that he didn't have a sense of humour after all.

"We'll have to get it examined," went on the Commissioner, stating the obvious.

"I thought you might arrange it, Sir. Our laboratories aren't quite set up for this kind of thing," Willy Best said, as he returned the leaden object to the table. He picked up the cutaway Bible, opening it in front of the Commissioner.

"Interesting idea. Using a priest on the verge of heart failure. Interesting people we've got to deal with," he added dryly.

Tehran, 10:30 A.M.

Anna Morgue, alias Félix, walked across the concrete apron to the waiting British Airways plane. All around her were a party of Iranian teenagers on their way to London. She had good friends in Iran who had arranged for her to travel in this party, which should make for no difficulty on her arrival in London. The same good friends had long since arranged an Iranian passport on her behalf. So all was well and calm. Except that the German, Hermann Kapp, would have some explaining to do. Sending out a three-point call would demand a satisfactory explanation, for it permitted no refusal except in great emergency. Besides which there was an unresolved "something" between herself and this Hermann Kapp. The German was clever, but she doubted he had much in his gut.

Anna Morgue was five-ten in height, with her auburn hair cut shorter than many men. Her forehead was high, her eyebrows rather fine and well separated, the eyes themselves a dark brown, but with the left one having a light fleck in the pupil. The nose was rather long and pointed, and the mouth small and often pursed. She was a woman of great energy, strength of will, and cunning, and, at the age of twenty-three, of strong sexuality. Her normal taste was for women a year or two younger than herself, but for a while after a personal killing her preference swung toward men.

Moscow, Noon

Igor Markov had managed to put off giving any report for almost two days. His operation in its early stages would have looked too grandiose, too theoretical. He wanted the flags to be moving in a convergent army toward the British Isles before discussing things in detail with Valas Georgian. And the near miss in Göteborg had been something of a shock. It wasn't until that morning, when he had heard with relief of the successful completion of the episode of the Volvo spares, that he had felt sufficient confidence to invite the General to his Babushkin office. Valas Georgian had driven out there by 11:30 A.M., and for the past hour and a half he had been listening to Markov with concealed admiration. He had learned about the four courier systems, one through Eire, one directly and easily from Libya to London, one through East Germany and Sweden, and one by car through Holland. The first and the last of these couriers had been carrying plutonium. The second and the third had been carrying enriched uranium—plutonium and enriched uranium both being bomb-making materials for nuclear devices.

Valas Georgian had learned of the separation of function between the courier systems and the ultimate bombmakers. He had been worried by the bomb-making team being in the charge of a certain German, Hermann Kapp. But how could it be otherwise? Igor Markov had asked. Had he not been cautioned to avoid involving Soviet embassies and the Soviet government itself in the technical

aspects of the operation? Igor Markov also pointed out
that the greatest reservoir of psychologically disturbed
persons was in West Germany, Sweden, and Britain. So
clearly it was such persons who had to be used. Valas
Georgian had nodded in reluctant agreement with this
analysis.

Lunch with a welcome drink had been brought in.
Then a stolid-faced bulky woman messenger walked
straight into the office holding a pink paper. Igor Markov
took one look at it and broke out instantly with the exple-
tive "Shit it all!" The stolid-faced woman permitted her
eyebrows to lift sharply, and as if a fireball had appeared
in the office, she raced for the door. Markov gave a mut-
tered apology to the General, for unlike some high officials in the Western democracies, high officials in the
Soviet Union did not habitually speak in such terms, even
in private in front of their wives and families. Indeed,
Igor Markov perceived that some satisfactory explanation
for his momentary lapse was essential, and this forced
him to reveal more than he would normally have done.
In dealing with a vodka-swilling bonehead like Valas
Georgian, it was advisable to keep explanations to a mini-
mum, but this he could do no longer, at any rate if he
was to preserve his reputation for finesse.

The true problem which had still to be faced, Markov
warned his superior, was to persuade the British of the
seriousness of the threat against them. The British notori-
ously were smug, self-satisfied people. What would be
the use of telling such a people that a nuclear bomb had
been placed in their midst, at the very nerve centre of
their country? Would they not just laugh and assert the
threat to be only bluff? So what could be done to convince
them otherwise, except actually to explode the bomb?
But this would be to destroy the whole mission, for the
issue was not to explode a bomb in London, but to prevent

a veto from being cast at the United Nations. This indeed was the very centre of the problem, Markov asserted with some gravity.

What he had done, he now explained, was to plan that two of his courier systems should be abortive, the couriers with the plutonium. For plutonium is not really a good bomb-making material, except for professionals. The real threat was to come from the highly enriched uranium, which was a much less difficult material to work with.

So he went on to explain about the Irish priest. Valas Georgian laughed to think of the Roman Church being involved in such a way. He complimented Igor Markov on the lunch, taking the opportunity to pour himself another snifter.

Now at last Markov came to the wretched courier from East Germany. He explained how he had taken good care to choose a broken-down fellow, a seedy man who would surely be intercepted ten times over. Yet such was the irony of events that the fellow had somehow got through successfully, whereas the carefully prepared linkages from East Berlin to Sassnitz, to Göteborg, to England, had come so near to foundering. Valas Georgian laughed still more uproariously at this failure of careful calculation, so much so that Markov thought it opportune to take a much larger slug of vodka than was his habit. The fiery liquid bit into his mouth and throat, invading his windpipe with its scorched earth. He erupted into furious coughing, and then lights flashed violently before his eyes as Georgian hit him carelessly on the back with a huge pawlike fist.

It would be several hours before Igor Markov would feel like thinking and plotting again, but when he did so a truly brilliant stroke concerning the pitiful agent from East Germany would occur to him. The stroke was so elegant that it needed only a simple message to the Englishman, Sunion Webb, to put it into operation.

Moyen Atlas, Morocco, 1 P.M.

The sheep put up a cloud of dust as they passed by the reclining man. As the shepherd himself went by, the reclining man, who had a broad hat across his face to shield his eyes from the afternoon sun, called a greeting in Berber. The dialect was the local one, so the shepherd continued on his way, convinced that here was no stranger ripe for the plucking.

Ten minutes later, the reclining man pulled the hat away from his eyes, sat upright, and then jammed the hat on his head, throwing his face once more into a shadow. In the brief moment of exposure in the bright sunlight the man could be seen to have smooth black hair, large black eyebrows, and a black moustache, the two ends of which curled downward around his mouth until they reached the line of the jawbone.

Abu l'Weifa, generally known as Pedro-the-Basque, had come up into the middle hills for the purpose of communing with himself. The shepherd who had just passed him by was more on his mind than the messenger from Fez who had sought him out during the morning. For the nomadic shepherd, living day to day in his black tent, was a symbol of the history of Morocco. It was a past that must inevitably soon be gone, to be replaced by what? The question had troubled Abu l'Weifa from his student days. He had studied a little economics while a student, enough to make him sharply aware of the boundlessly rising population, a population more fertile than the land itself, of the potential mineral riches, and of his country's chronic lack of capital. In Abu l'Weifa's eyes this had not added up to a peaceful future for his country. From the beginning he had rejected the comfortable life of the civil servant, because his father and uncle were civil servants, and he could easily see for himself that the pathway there did not lead to any mountain summit.

He had thought about joining a group of dissidents, but his natural intelligence had warned him that this too would be ineffective. The group was too undisciplined, too unskilled, to be any threat to the established regime. Besides, history showed that successful revolutionary movements come either from the army or from outside. The army not being to his taste, he had therefore moved across the narrow entrance of the Mediterranean into Spain, back to the land which his distant Moorish forebears had once controlled. It had been through firearms that the Spaniards had driven out his ancestors, so it was to explosives that Abu l'Weifa had naturally turned, to repay the Spaniards in kind.

Over the years, nearly ten years now, he had become an operator of the highest international class. From time to time he returned quietly to Morocco, to see how things were looking, to see if the time seemed ripe. As his experience increased, and as the established regime lurched from one economic crisis to the next, the time was clearly becoming more and more ripe, to a point where Abu l'Weifa was beginning to wonder if the time might not be overripe. And this was one of the two reasons why he had troubled himself to ride up here into the mountains, to commune with himself.

The other reason was the mundane one that the situation in Spain was currently hot. Two months ago Abu l'Weifa had achieved the impossible. He had blown up two members of the Spanish government in full daylight in a main street of Madrid, in spite of the police escort which had accompanied the ministers' cars. Like the best tricks of an expert conjurer it had been done in the most blatant fashion. Once the route which the vehicles were to take was known, the method had been simple. Thirty workmen had arrived at a suitable point on the route, and had begun to dig up the side of the road. They had been equipped with a concrete mixer, compressed air generator, an earth-shifting machine, all very impressive. By the time they were noticed by the police they had spiked a water main, which they were then proceeding to repair. The police stayed around after that, watching in a casual kind of way. But the casual watching of the comings and goings of thirty men had not prevented the best part of half a ton of explosives being planted there, together with a battery and detonator. Abu l'Weifa was particularly proud of the detonating device. A wire from the detonator had gone to one of the sidewalk grilles, and near its end it had been taped to the underside of the grille. The wire actually ended in a photocell which had a little black hood over it. All that had to be done to explode the charge was to stand beside the grille and remove the black hood. Sunlight did the rest, and a twenty-foot crater appeared in the road with the cars all crumpled around it. Abu l'Weifa gave a harsh but still rather musical chuckle whenever he happened to think about it.

The disadvantage of such an operation was that afterward something just had to give. Too many people had been involved. Weeks of police probing would be certain to turn up something. One or more of the "workmen" would be arrested, and bit by bit the trail would gradually lead to Abu l'Weifa himself, or as the police would think, to Pedro-the-Basque. For it would be Pedro, with his well-learned Basque slang, for whom the police would be searching, far to the north in the back streets of Bilbao. Abu l'Weifa again gave his curious chuckle at the thought of such stupidity.

Then the messenger from Fez had come, with the three-point request from Paris. A three-point request meant there would be good money. Not that Abu l'Weifa had much use for money as such. But with money one

could equip oneself with the tools of one's trade. Money
was an unfortunate necessity, and so it had to be picked
up whenever it was freely available. With a sigh of regret,
for he would have like to spend several more days up
there on the mountain ridge, Abu l'Weifa walked in no
great hurry—it was remarkable how quickly he always
slipped back into the slow measured pace of his real fellow
countrymen—to a clump of wild olive trees. From out
of the coarse esparto grass where it had been hidden
from the passing shepherd he lifted up his bike and swung
a leg over the saddle. A quick kick on the starter and
the Kawasaki engine burst into life. He pulled up the
side stand, selected low gear, and began the journey that
would take him first to Fez, then to Tangiers, and thence
quite simply, in a plane jam-packed with summer tourists,
to London.

St. John's Wood, 2 P.M.

Colonel Barry Gwent of Military Intelligence stood in
front of Willy Best's desk. He had come to St. John's Wood
in uniform, because he had expected the police also to
be in uniform. But Willy Best sat there at his desk in
slacks and a casual shirt, the sleeves rolled to the elbows.
This made Barry Gwent feel awkward, especially with
the red tabs on his shoulder straps and on his beret. He
was thirty-five years old, in excellent physical condition,
for he was a keen mountaineer and rock climber. He
had a thatch of black hair, well trimmed, but a thatch
for all that.

"I thought Sir Stanley Farrar was to be here," Gwent
began.

Willy Best allowed himself a slight smile at the half
insult. It was his temperament that made it easy for him

to maintain his smile and to reply in a friendly voice, "He'll be along soon. He phoned to say he'd been delayed."

"Then perhaps we'd better wait."

"We can wait, or you can tell me what you've found." Willy Best looked down at the desk, fiddled with a pencil, and continued with the smile still playing around the corners of his mouth, "Look, Colonel Gwent, you wouldn't have come round here yourself if it hadn't been important. I know you'd rather speak to the Commissioner . . ."

"It's my job to speak to the Commissioner. If I don't . . ."

"He might be annoyed at finding us talking together before he gets here," finished Best. "But he won't be. He's not that kind."

As the man at the desk calmly lifted his grey eyes, Barry Gwent made a sudden decision.

"Well," he said, "we found plutonium."

Willy Best lowered his head again and went back to fiddling with the pencil, turning it over and over with only one hand.

"I was afraid you might," he nodded.

"We were told it had come in from Eire."

"Yes," answered Best, contriving to make the single syllable last for an unconscionably long time.

"It would be interesting to know how it got to Eire."

"Interesting for you. It's what it might be doing here that interests us. How much was there?"

"I knew you'd come to that. I'm not really supposed to say."

"Not even to Sir Stanley."

"Not even to Sir Stanley. But strictly between ourselves, it was about one-third of what would be needed."

"To make a bomb?"

"Yes." It was Barry Gwent's turn to make the syllable long-lasting.

"Then we must start looking for the other two-thirds."

Gwent was suprised at the policeman's calm.

"I'll be glad to do what I can," he said.

"Tell me, Colonel Gwent, is it easy to make such a bomb?"

"To make a plutonium bomb that would be of military significance is really quite hard. To make a bomb that would be significant to a terrorist would not be nearly so difficult. Assuming they didn't destroy themselves first."

"Could the IRA do it?"

Gwent stood almost at attention, slightly shaking his head.

"That's a hard question, Superintendent, because you never quite know who might be working for the IRA. The answer could be yes, if they have well-trained university men working for them."

"We'd better start looking for university graduates, as well as the rest of that plutonium," Willy Best said, getting up from the desk. "Colonel Gwent, you've been a great help. I'll be getting back to you as soon as we have any information," he said, holding out a hand.

"But how about Sir Stanley?" Gwent was surprised at how big Best's hand was for so slender a man, big and hard, horny, you might say.

"The Commissioner is in a meeting. I'm going there now, to pull him out of it. Come with me if you wish."

Monza, Italy, 3 P.M.

"What is it?" Al Simmonds had roared ten hours earlier from inside his tent.

"Telephone," a child's voice had shouted back at him.
"Where from?" he had asked.

"Paris," was the high-pitched reply.

So he'd quickly pulled faded blue overalls on top of
his pyjamas and had gone off to listen to what Paris had
to offer. The call was from Louis-le-Poisson. As soon as
he heard the curious overtones of Louis' voice he'd
shaken the mists of sleep from his mind. He'd heard the
offer and had then gone back to the tent. Everybody
who worked with Al Simmonds said he was a calm cookie,
and anybody who knew what a three-point job meant,
and who had watched Al Simmonds slip off his overalls,
get back into his sleeping bag, and fall asleep again, really
asleep, would not have doubted the description.

Although he had been noncommittal on the phone,
Al Simmonds knew perfectly well that a three-point job
could not be refused whatever it might be, and Louis
had known it too. Such jobs were just too profitable. So
on waking he set about packing up. The gang would just
have to do without him in the racing pit for the rest of
the week. After breakfast he rang Monique. There was
a long pause, from which he guessed that she had spent
the night with someone, the bloody whore. Why did he
always get himself shacked up with that sort of girl, he
wondered? He told her he would be away from Milan
for a few days, and he tried to tell from her voice whether
she was concerned or not. She asked him where he was
going, and he said across the border into Switzerland,
which was true enough because he intended to go by
the afternoon train, through Switzerland by Brigue and
Geneva to Paris and London.

Al Simmonds was small but broad with little excess
fat about him. His arms and hands were exceedingly
strong, so strong that he could easily have broken a man's
neck with them, had he been of a mind to do so. But

that was hardly his style, unless he had come to it over
a girl. And with those hands he had made a lot of things
in his forty-one years. The things he had made were not
of outstanding aesthetic quality, like a fine picture or a
piece of sculpture, but they always had the great merit
of working smoothly, of doing exactly the job they were
supposed to do. His life was like that, never hitting the
high spots but always running along like a smoothly functioning machine. Not much went wrong for Al Simmonds,
especially when there was good money to be made from
time to time. It was only a matter of seeing ahead just
a little all the time, and of then easing yourself carefully
and sensibly over any obstacles that might happen to
lie in your path.

It was coming up to 3 P.M. when Simmonds mounted
his bicycle and pedalled away from Monza with a small
rucksack on his back. It took a little longer on the bike
than a car or taxi would have done to make the ten-
odd miles into Milan. But this way he travelled easily
and silently, a ghost, you might say, among the noisy
traffic. By 4 P.M. he had booked tickets to London for
himself and his bike, he had made sure the bike was
suitably stored on the train, and he had walked through
the train itself, searching for the compartment with the
most attractive-looking female in it.

Whitehall, 5 P.M.

Henry Fielding, the Home Secretary, was a tall, dark,
studious-looking man with less of a weight problem than
most of his Cabinet colleagues. He wore thin black horn-
rimmed spectacles, and his slightly greying hair was carefully combed back over the high crown of his head.

"You are quite sure of this?" he asked when Sir Stanley
Farrar, the Metropolitan Police Commissioner, had told

him of the intercepted plutonium. "I knew about the Irish priest of course," he added. "Awkward business, but a little less awkward now, I suppose."

"We're sure about it," said Farrar in a heavy style which Willy Best, who stood there beside him, could not have matched. The Commissioner, with his huge, tall figure, always seemed to Willy Best to be two men, one from the waist upward, the other from the waist downward.

"We're putting on a full-scale drive to find the rest of the plutonium," Sir Stanley continued.

"Do that," agreed the Home Secretary. Then he went into a brown study, emerging to say, "What I can't really see is what the IRA can demand, I mean, if they could get a bomb into London."

"The withdrawal of the army from the north of Ireland," Sir Stanley suggested.

"Agreed," the Home Secretary answered immediately, "but I don't see how the government could possibly accept such a demand."

"I don't quite see how you work that one out, Sir." Willy Best was surprised to hear the sound of his own voice. He had come to the meeting feeling that supers should be seen and not heard.

"Well, the government couldn't possibly agree to blackmail of that order. The IRA must know that we couldn't."

"Actually, Sir, there may be a point in your favour," Willy Best plunged on desperately.

Both the Commissioner and the Home Secretary directed their full attention at the Super, Sir Stanley feeling glad that a point could be found in favour of the Home Secretary.

"Well, it's just that I wouldn't have done it that way."

"Meaning what?"

"Well, I wouldn't have used a priest on the verge of heart failure."

"And who would you have used?"

"Well, if I'd wanted to smuggle such a thing into the U.K., I'd have used a priest who wasn't on the verge of heart failure."

"Perhaps they didn't know he was," the Home Secretary suggested, combing his hair with his hand.

Marble Arch, London, 6:30 A.M.

Over the past hour the desk clerk at the Cumberland Hotel had checked in more than fifty new guests. He remembered quite a few of them, but his memory would be short-lived, necessarily so, for even if it had been his job it would have been an exceedingly difficult task to remember in any permanent way the several hundred people each day who checked into the hotel. But for the moment at least he would have remembered the big fair-haired man with the tinted glasses, the one he thought at first to be American, but who had then spoken to him in a German accent. He would have remembered the dark-skinned man, the one with the moustache down to the jawline. And the tall auburn-haired woman who looked like a model. But it was typical that the desk clerk had no memory of Al Simmonds, for Simmonds had a way of moving in or out without people noticing him at all. Yet Al Simmonds too had arrived, on the same train, as it happened, with Hermann Kapp. It was also typical that Simmonds had noticed the German, but the German had not noticed him—perhaps the young fellow had trouble with the tinted glasses, Al Simmonds thought. Al Simmonds had made no contact with the German because that was not the way of it. Only trouble could come from breaking well-tried rules.

Although the desk clerk could for the moment have remembered three of the four of them, his memory would be evanescent. By tomorrow it would be faint, by the day after tomorrow it would be vestigial, and by the day after that it would be gone.

Downing Street, 9 P.M.

Henry Fielding, the Home Secretary, had long since learned that to look foolish never did a politician any real harm, except possibly at the time of an election. It was things which took money out of the pockets of his constituents that did the real damage. For this sound reason he habitually permitted himself to seem more stupid than he really was. He had not been in the least difficulty to understand the seriousness of the police discoveries, and no sooner had the Commissioner and the Super quitted his office than he had been through to the Prime Minister. The Prime Minister had agreed to see him at nine o'clock, and nine o'clock found him promptly on the steps of number 10. Big Ben was striking just as one of the two policemen on duty there showed him inside the Prime Minister's residence.

He made his way upstairs to the Prime Minister's office, and within a matter of a few moments the two of them were sipping glasses of Scotch whiskey. Henry Fielding came straight to the point, and since there was not so far very much to tell, it took him only a short while to tell it. The Prime Minister listened, his face a glowing moon of fellowship and good cheer. When the Home Secretary had finished, he leaned forward in his chair, as if to rivet the listener's attention, and said with a spreading confidential smile, "You know, Henry, I've always thought that if I were a terrorist that's exactly what I would do myself."

The Home Secretary smoothed his hair from his forehead to the nape of his neck. "But what should we do? That is the question."

" 'Whether it be nobler in the mind . . .'," the Prime

Minister nodded, his kindly eyes atwinkle.

"The police think there's more of the stuff to be found,"
the Home Secretary gulped.

"Then let them find it. Come now, Henry, what would
be the use of you and me starting to look? We wouldn't
know where to begin. Buying ourselves deerstalker hats
and magnifying glasses. Oh, dear me, no. How ridiculous
it would be."

"Then you think I should do nothing?"

The Prime Minister's aura of bonhomie seemed to ex-
pand ever further. "By no means, Henry. You must do
something about the Irish priest. You must write a letter
of condolence to his bishop and to his family—if he had
one."

"I might do *what!*" the Home Secretary exploded into
his glass.

"Of course you must. Think of it as a useful test of
your ability to dissemble. If you make a good job of it,
the IRA will probably think that we haven't found the
plutonium."

The Prime Minister put down his glass. It was time
to get rid of Henry Fielding, he had decided. Not from
the Cabinet or from his office, but out of his house. His
own time, he felt, could now be better occupied.

"I'm not one given to unnecessary compliments," he
said, "but I wish everyone would do what you've just
done. I mean, coming here and telling me about your
problem straightaway, not delaying until months afterward. It makes my job less difficult. Thank you, Henry."

With this valedictory offering he stood up, moved
firmly to the door, and bowed out the Home Secretary.
As soon as he was satisfied that Fielding had indeed gone,
the Prime Minister went with a determined step immediately to the telephone.

Washington, D.C., 5:30 P.M.

The President marched to the Oval Office, a half-smoked cigar held between his lips.

"It seems as if the British have got the snake pit all stirred up," he announced to Heisal Woods, the Secretary of State. "I've just had a call from the Prime Minister," he added.

"About what?"

"IRA smuggling plutonium into the country."

Heisal Woods scratched his head vigourously, and then said, "You know, Chief, my old father had a saying which impressed my young mind. He was an engineer. When a piece of machinery went wrong, with all manner of troubles showing themselves, he used to say that it's rare for there to be more than one criminal in the household."

The President relit his dormant cigar.

"You mean our Soviet friends are still with us?"

"That's what I would say."

"Any suggestions?"

Woods scratched his head again, causing his eyeglasses to bounce on his nose.

"Turn the information we have on IRA-Soviet relations over to the British," he suggested.

"Touché," grinned the President, blowing out a cloud of smoke, making Heisal Woods wonder if he cared a longshoreman's jump about the state of his lungs. As if the President had pressed a button there was a knock on the office door. In response to a yell from the President, a grey-haired man of middle height entered the room. His face had an intrinsically serious composure to it, emphasized by the thin steel-rimmed glasses that he wore. He looked fit, and as Robert Becker, the head of the CIA, told his friends, he felt fit.

"We were just talking about you, and about turning

IRA files over to the British," the President remarked.

"No way," was Becker's uncompromising reply.

For answer the President burst into a roar of laughter, taking a fresh cigar from the box on his desk. Then, after his usual biting routine, he lit it with a very large match which he struck with a kind of stabbing motion against a rough surface on the side of his desk.

"You were saying, Bob?" the President continued in an amiable tone.

"I'm saying that no IRA files leave my office. If the British care to send somebody over here, I'm willing to let them go through what we've got. But as to our sending anything to London, absolutely not."

"No telling what might become of it, eh?"

"No telling at all. Before we can turn around, somebody relays the whole thing to Dublin. That's the way it goes."

"You never know where the ripples stop?"

"Never."

Heisal Woods listened to this interchange. Thinking he'd better make his presence known, he said, "Well, Bob, that seems to me like a sensible offer. But who is going to tell the British?"

"I am," grunted the President. "I'm going to tell their Prime Minister. What hips me about him is how a guy like that, with a moon face and a Sunday-afternoon smile, comes out top of the pops all the time. Maybe I should start practising."

The President, cigar still in his mouth, screwed up his face in what was a barely passable imitation of the British Prime Minister, and the two other men grinned with him as they prepared to return to their own departments.

London, 10:45 P.M.

For the past two hours Sunion Webb had kept glancing every few minutes at his watch. From the moment of his return from 17A Courtlane Mews he had remained at the Cumberland Hotel, closeted in his room, with food brought up to him from time to time. He had done this, not because he wanted to do so, but because his instructions had been emphatic on this point. Moving about in the streets or even in the hotel lobby could achieve no advantage, and it could all too easily bring chance recognition from one of his many acquaintances. Chance meetings happen all too often, and sometimes when they are least wanted.

From the moments of their individual arrivals, Hermann Kapp, Anna Morgue, Abu l'Weifa, and Al Simmonds had all remained in their rooms, widely separated from each other on the many floors of the hotel. They had all made use of room service for their evening meal. A young man dressed in the hotel uniform had also delivered a package weighing about five pounds to Anna Morgue. It contained a Browning pistol together with four clips of 9-mm ammunition. The pistol was obviously one of the many surplus models to be found floating around the international scene, but it was in satisfactory condition, and Anna Morgue had learned her craft with one.

Since airlines all over the world had greatly tightened up their security precautions, it had become foolish for high-grade operators like Anna Morgue to carry weapons of any kind on ordinary commercial flights. Movements by rail and by sea were therefore now to be preferred, but in this case time had been much too short for that. So the service offered by Louis-le-Poisson had proved its value once more. Maybe Louis was even worth the money he was paid, Anna Morgue permitted herself to think. After carefully testing the pressure on the trigger mechanism, she put the pistol into its box, which she stowed away in her handgrip together with the ammunition clips. She stuffed the soft packing material into a plastic bag, which she also squeezed into the handgrip.

Through being closeted so long in his room, Sunion Webb had come to realise that he was now involved in a practical operation, and it was this which was making him increasingly nervous. To begin with, Igor Markov's plan had been only a theoretical design, an abstraction in Webb's mind, an abstraction like the intricacies of Karl Marx's writings. But now he had a real, practical thing to do. He had to contact the hotel telephone girl, to find out if a Mr. Kapp had arrived there. The agreed time had been 10:55 P.M. It was the fine detail of it, 10:55, not 11, which was making Sunion Webb nervous. It was things like having to set his watch by the BBC 9 P.M. signal that were worrying him, for in this world of brief-cases with their deadly content, of time judged to a fraction of a minute, he was a fish out of water.

But the contact with Hermann Kapp was made easily enough, so easily that Sunion Webb felt angry with himself for his own flaccid mentality. At 11 P.M. exactly he quitted his room, took the elevator down to the hotel lobby, went outside the hotel, walked the streets for a while, returned at 11:15 P.M., and took the same elevator as before. He punched the button for the topmost floor, not because his room was on that floor, but because the several people in the elevator were likely to quit it at the intermediate levels. Which they did, leaving Hermann Kapp and himself together for a moment at the top. Sunion Webb realised that the German had waited in the lobby until he had returned from his brief stroll outside the hotel, and had then simply moved into the same elevator, along with several other genuine strangers. The contact had thus been straightforward, and in the brief moment before the elevator started downward again, Webb told Kapp that the "safe" house was to be 17A Courtlane Mews. Then he quitted the elevator himself at his own floor, leaving the German to his own devices.

It was now Hermann Kapp's turn to make the appropriate contacts. He rode the elevator back down to the ground floor, and immediately made contact with Anna Morgue on the house phone from the lobby. A few minutes later she appeared in the lobby herself, and the German told her about Al Simmonds and about Courtlane Mews. Anna Morgue then returned to her room and put through a brief call to Simmonds, who appeared himself soon thereafter in the lobby to receive similar information from Hermann Kapp. The process was repeated for Abu l'Weifa, with Simmonds now making the contact on the house phone. Thus the house phone was used only once each by Hermann Kapp, Anna Morgue, and Al Simmonds, and not at all by Abu l'Weifa, whose accent might have been remembered by the operator.

There was a good reason for arranging the contact in this way. Sunion Webb was the primary organiser, and contact had to go from him to Hermann Kapp, the secondary organiser. And the contacts had to go from Kapp to each of the other three because it was Hermann Kapp who had himself activated the other three. The progression was from higher to lower in the structure of the plan because in this way the lower could never implicate the higher. If Hermann Kapp had suspected that he was under surveillance of any kind, he would not have responded to the call from Sunion Webb, and if Anna Morgue, Al Simmonds, or Abu l'Weifa had felt themselves to be under any observation or suspicion, they too would not have responded. Not only did this one-way system for the transmission of information protect the upper levels of the plan, but by keeping the crucial initial information away from the lower levels, it indirectly protected the lower levels as well.

The Construction Begins

Washington, D.C., Noon

Willy Best emerged from the gate of the Eastern Airlines
flight from New York. He walked into the rotunda of
Washington National Airport carrying only a small hand-
case, feeling punch-drunk by the pace of events. He had
been awakened out of an uneasy sleep at 4:30 that morning by the Commissioner who had told him to get out
to Heathrow by 5:45, to catch an early plane to New
York. The Commissioner had been astonishingly vague
about the purpose of the trip. Beyond instructing him
to find out anything the Americans had got, there was
little else that Sir Stanley could tell him. Almost as an
afterthought Best had asked where in America was he
to go? The United States was a big country, and until
he had landed in New York at 9:15 local time he hadn't
really appreciated just how big it really was. The Commissioner had told him to go to Washington and so here
he was in Washington, looking for somebody who was
supposed to meet him. The steward on the plane into
New York had checked timetables for him and told him
to take a taxi from Kennedy Airport to La Guardia, which

he had done. From La Guardia he had caught the New York-to-Washington shuttle, and all the time he was bemused by why everything seemed so different from London, even though the language was the same. It seemed more different than Paris or Rome or Vienna.

And how was he to find the somebody who was supposed to meet him? But someone did meet him, a young fair-haired chap who identified himself as having come from the British Embassy. The moment he and the young man emerged from the main exit a car of American manufacture drew in close by the sidewalk. The young fellow opened a door and Best climbed inside.

The chauffeur whisked them along a wide boulevard into the city centre. There the fast progress came to an abrupt stop, however. Although the driver was quick to seize any opening in the heavy traffic, it was a further thirty-five minutes before he drew the car in at a tall glass-and-concrete building. Willy Best had assumed he was to be taken to the embassy itself. But he had not asked about it. He had contented himself with small talk because he hadn't wanted to appear ignorant about the purpose of his visit. So he was in some surprise when the young man took him inside the glass-and-concrete building, handling him on to a well-dressed woman of about thirty-five who was expecting him.

Willy Best was aware that there is a moment up to which you can ask a question without seeming impossibly foolish, and beyond which you cannot. Just as there is a moment up to which you can ask a person's name, and beyond which you cannot. So putting on his most disarming smile, he said, "You know, Miss, it's probably the silliest question you've ever heard, but where am I?"

The woman laughed, and then put her finger up to her lips. "Shush," she whispered mockingly, "this is the CIA." It was Willy Best's turn to laugh.

"They just told me to come to Washington, not who I was to see."

"You mean you've just come from England?"

Best nodded, and the woman added, "Poor man."

By this time she had conducted him to an office with a card slotted on the door which read Mrs. Jane Barrow. Since the woman led him straight into the office, it seemed probable that Jane Barrow was her name, but the moment for asking about it had now passed by. Although the room was large, it was obviously a secretary's office, and Best had long since learned that the only secretaries with large offices are those who serve important persons. This proved true, for the woman took him to a communicating door which led into a still larger office, which plainly was not secretarial.

"Police Superintendent Best to see you," the woman said. A grey-haired man wearing thin steel-rimmed spectacles rose from a distant desk. He came toward Best offering his hand.

"Bob Becker," he announced.

There was a momentary sparkle in Willy Best's eyes as he shook hands. "Mr. Becker, it's very good of you to see me like this. Very good indeed."

As he spoke, Willy Best was oddly conscious that his speech suddenly had more of his native Somerset in it than he would ever have used back in London.

"Superintendent, I'm going to apologise right away for not being as cooperative as you might expect, or as I'd like to be," said Becker.

"I'll be happy to leave you to decide, Sir."

"It's this way. I've been asked to show you the contents of certain files. They're laid out on the table over there. If you have any questions about them, Jane will help. I'm going to be out of the office myself, but I'll see you again before you leave."

"May I take notes?" Willy Best asked, pointing to his case.

"As you like, but leave them with Jane. We'll see to it that they're delivered promptly to you in London. It's just that I don't want you, or anybody else, carrying the information in those files about with them here in the United States. If anything came out, the Irish section of our population wouldn't like it. Back in London, it's none of my concern. Don't misunderstand me, Superintendent. I'm not suggesting any carelessness on your part, but accidents happen—like an accident on the highway— and I don't take any stock in accidents myself."

With a short bow, Becker then left the room. Except that he didn't have whiskers and muttonchops, he reminded Best of a Victorian gentleman. Jane Barrow, as her name evidently was, came in and started to show him the way the files had been ordered. Then she was concerned to know whether he had an adequate supply of paper and pencils, and Best began to think that Mr. Barrow was a lucky man.

In fact, Jane Barrow was divorced, and in fact she had herself been immediately attracted by this strange policeman with a quizzical smile and a twinkle in his eye. She had never seen, or even conceived, that a policeman could be like this. Policemen and intelligence men were always so serious in her experience, steely-eyed and pointed-jawed, as one might say. Jane Barrow left the connecting door into the main office open, and as she sat there she listened in further surprise to the grunts, exclamations, and chuckles of Willy Best as he glanced rapidly through the pile of files which lay on the table before him.

There was a triple fascination for Willy Best in looking through those files, a fascination over the bits which overlapped what he knew already to be true, a fascination over some things which he knew to be untrue, and a fascination over things that were entirely different from anything he had seen before. It was about these last things that he mostly made notes, scribbling them rapidly on the sheets of paper Jane Barrow had given him. He also made a list of items which seemed doubtful to him, which he would leave there for Bob Becker to make what use of he pleased.

Best was sensitive enough to understand that he had but the afternoon hours to check through the formidable pile of files. These people didn't want him around, not for a moment longer than was necessary. Besides which it was important for him to be back in London as soon as possible, particularly so in view of a few important points he was gleaning as he went along. So he worked hard and fast in spite of the fatigue that was beginning to creep up on him.

It was coming 6 P.M. when Bob Becker returned to the office. As he came in, Willy Best rose from the table.

"Well, Mr. Becker," he said, "that's been most interesting."

"Find anything?"

"Yes, as a matter of fact, I did. Among the Soviet connections. We're not strong on that kind of material. I suppose because it's considered a bit too diplomatic for the police to handle."

"Look, I've got a sandwich and a bottle of beer in one of the other rooms. You can come back afterward if you want to."

"No, I've had a fair whack at it. I'd like to be getting back to London as soon as I can."

"Suppose you give Jane your airline ticket. She'll check the flights that are going out tonight."

The sandwich and the bottle of beer turned out to be something of an understatement. There was cold salmon and chicken, fruit, and a multitude of drinks. Willy Best decided on a glass of chilled white wine.

"Can I ask about the latest press reports?" he said. "I mean, has there been any press report about the plutonium?"

"Why would you British announce it?"

"We wouldn't, but the IRA might."

"No, there's been nothing through on the wire."

Willy Best smiled in a shy way as he ate the salmon, as if he were reluctant to offer his opinions in such high-powered company.

"Can I put it directly to you, Mr. Becker? Do you think this plutonium is really IRA work?"

"Well I'd begin by asking where they got it from. No doubt you have."

"I have thought about it, yes."

"With what conclusion?"

"I don't think the IRA has enough money to buy the stuff, not on the market—if there is such a thing as a market. So I think they must have been supplied with it. And then I keep asking myself who might have done the supplying."

"Any conclusion on that?"

"Not very definitely," Best said, looking down at his plate.

Robert Becker thought for a while, and then took the plunge. "Have you considered there might be a connection with the South African sanctions motion in the UN Security Council?"

Still looking down at his plate, Willy Best thought it might be tactless to say that the possibility had indeed occurred to him.

"That's the most interesting suggestion I've heard," he said in a tone of some enthusiasm. "You know, Sir, I wonder if there's something you'd do for me—as well as the help you've already given me," he finished hastily.

"What might that be?"

"To pass the word through to H.M. government that this might have some connection with the UN business. I don't know just how much ordinary police work you see in your department, Mr. Becker, but there are plenty of people who take every advantage to spread false scare stories. So that governments get themselves into the habit of thinking it's all just 'cry wolf'," Willy Best explained.

A phone rang, which Becker answered.

"That was Jane," he said. "She tells me you could catch a direct flight from Dulles to London if you can leave here in the next few minutes. I don't want to push you, of course. Take all the time you like. And I'll have a word about the UN connection."

"I've already taken too much of your day, Mr. Becker."

"Jane will see that you get to the airport, then."

"It's very kind of you. And thanks for the salmon, it was delicious."

A moment later Willy Best found himself following Jane Barrow out of the glass-and-concrete building, much as he had done on the way in, except that Jane was now wearing a short outdoor coat. A car was waiting, but not with the chauffeur. Jane herself slipped into the driver's seat.

"I'm taking you out to the airport myself," she said.

Willy Best felt curiously embarrassed as he sat there, particularly as the drive out to the airport seemed much longer than the drive in had been. When he asked about it, Jane Barrow explained "Oh, there are two airports. Dulles takes the big planes and it's about thirty miles out."

For most of the journey he felt tongue-tied, which was unusual for him. But try as he would, he could think of nothing sensible to say. They parked the car and walked together to the passenger entrance gates.

"It's boarding," Jane Barrow said, "but you have time."
Then they shook hands, and Willy Best thanked her for
all the help she had been. A moment later he had gone
into the curious shuttle vehicle that would take him across
the apron to the waiting plane. Jane Barrow returned
to her car, eased it out onto the highway, and started
back to Washington. Another day of her life had gone.

London, 8 A.M.

Sunion Webb was in a bright, energetic mood. Having
made his contact successfully with Hermann Kapp on
the previous evening, he was determined to make a successful showing of the rest of the operation. He took
breakfast at 7:30 A.M. in the hotel dining room, at which
hour there were quite a few tourists around, but fortunately not the kind of people who might recognise him.
Then he checked out, paying his bill at the cashier's grille.
Carrying the same bag he had used in Moscow, he walked
the short distance to the Marble Arch station and took
the underground to Gloucester Road. By 8:25 A.M. he
was at 17A Courtlane Mews to find the elderly couple
with their bags packed. The couple left shortly after his
arrival, and Sunion Webb saw them off at the door, ex-
pressing his hope that the weather would be fine for their
holiday. All very smoothly done, he thought. Then he
went through into the kitchen quarters to check that
the house was amply provisioned. There was a good store
of bread and cakes, tea and coffee, eggs and milk, but
he could find no meat. This had seemed a nuisance until
he remembered seeing a freezer in the workshop. So
he went down to the basement, stumbling about a little
until he found the electric light switches. To his satisfaction there was a more-than-ample supply of meat in the

freezer, and also to his satisfaction he noticed the second briefcase which the grey-haired caretaker had brought from King's Cross on the previous day. He opened up the briefcase, finding there a flat, yellow-packaged heavy object similar to the one in the briefcase which he himself had brought from the Libyan Embassy. Sunion Webb felt he had come a long way since his meeting only a few days earlier with Igor Markov in Babushkin, indeed a long way since his contact with Hermann Kapp on the boat in Amsterdam.

Sitting beside the briefcase he also found an unstamped typed letter addressed to himself. He read the contents, which were quite extensive, with great interest. As he returned upstairs he found himself a little overwhelmed at the subtlety of it all. This last detail was a real gem which no ponderous bourgeois society could possibly have imagined. Webb found himself even in some awe at this further indication of the profound intellectual quality of those who were standing behind him in this enterprise. It gave him an added surge of confidence.

Hermann Kapp, Al Simmonds, Abu l'Weifa, and Anna Morgue checked separately and at different times out of the Cumberland Hotel, and they made their way separately to 17A Courtlane Mews. Although they moved separately, their thoughts as they walked the last quarter of a mile to the house were the same. The whole district was thronged with a motley and polyglot crowd of people amongst whom they themselves must look very nondescript.

Anna Morgue was the last to arrive, for the good reason that she was the most likely one of the four to have been noticed as she came through immigration on the previous evening. To minimise this not-too-serious possibility she had stayed back at the hotel until close to midday, breakfasting in a leisurely way in her room. This had given ample opportunity for Louis-le-Poisson's agents to send her warning if the police should be nosing around the hotel. And all the time, from the moment she had left her room to the moment she turned into Courtlane Mews, she had kept her own sharp eyes wide open.

Hermann Kapp, Al Simmonds, and Abu l'Weifa had all gone down to the basement. Each had looked around there with attention to his own expertise. Simmonds had quickly tested the mechanical equipment. A few deft flicks at switches and levers, a few turnings of screws and knobs, had been sufficient. Then he had checked on quantities of sheet metal, bars, and rods, and also on a direct exit from the workshop, up a short flight of stone steps into a small yard which gave onto the street. Simmonds always concerned himself with the ins and outs of any new place.

Abu l'Weifa's examination of the workshop was less extensive. Inside the freezer he found four steel canisters each about eight inches across and eight inches high. Set out together on a bench they looked like the four pistons of some enormous engine. It took a little while for him to get one of them open. Then as he examined the dark brown material inside the open canister he gave his hoarse musical chuckle. Immediately he replaced the lid, and after making sure of its being airtight again, he replaced the four canisters in the freezer. Abu L'Weifa felt he had enough material to blow a sizable crater, just as he had done a few weeks ago in Madrid.

Hermann Kapp had glanced rather briefly at the workshop's electronics equipment. It was fully adequate for the job, he quickly decided, although it was no research laboratory. His main interest was in the contents of the two briefcases. The one in the safe contained a file of seven pages, as well as a yellow-packaged heavy, flat object. It was the file that occupied Kapp's attention. He

had laughed in relief to discover that the heavy material
consisted of highly enriched uranium, not plutonium,
which made the job far less difficult than he had feared.
There would be no problems of plutonium poisoning and
no need for fancy-shaped charges in the detonation system. An ordinary detonation velocity would be enough
to fire the two pieces of uranium toward each other, and
such a detonation would be an easy job for Pedro-the-
Basque. The one real complexity was the neutron source.
But then there were full instructions in the file about
the solution of that problem. And the material of the
neutron source was there too. It consisted of an α-active
substance, probably an isotope of radium, Hermann Kapp
thought, separated from a little boron by a sheet of low-
melting-point foil. Neutrons would come off as soon as
the foil was punctured or melted.

The flat pieces of uranium were not in the right shape,
of course. Hermann Kapp unpacked one of them. Simmonds and Pedro came to watch him as he examined
it carefully. It was a flat square of very heavy metal which
was made up of some sixty small cubes which had
been glued firmly together. Once unstuck, the cubes
could simply be reglued into a hemispheric form. Taking
great care to keep it well apart from the first piece of
uranium, Hermann Kapp then examined the second
piece, to find it also was made up of a similar array
of cubes. Clearly, then, they would simply build two hemi-
spheres of uranium within two steel cups that would serve
as neutron reflectors. One of the steel cups would be
fixed rigidly inside a metal cylinder, and the other cup
would be arranged to slide within the cylinder like a
hemispheric-domed piston. This movable piece would be
fired against the fixed piece, so that the uranium came
to form itself into a sphere. The neutron source would
be fastened to the fixed piece. When collision of the two

pieces occurred, the metal foil in the source would be destroyed, neutrons would be generated from the boron, and then the first neutrons would instantly be violently amplified by the resulting fission of the uranium.

There were no instructions in the file for the building of the explosive system that would drive the movable piece of uranium into the fixed piece. Nor were there instructions concerning the electronic method to be used to initiate the whole thing. But then, of course, no instructions were really needed, since Pedro and Hermann Kapp himself were fully skilled in these matters.

Sunion Webb came downstairs to tell them in a cheerful voice that lunch was ready. The lunch turned out to be a pile of overcooked chops, which Al Simmonds, who was himself an excellent cook, ate in sour silence. Webb, unconscious that his theoretical approach to such a thoroughly practical matter was not appreciated, asked how long the job downstairs would take. Hermann Kapp gave him a short and accurate estimate, twenty-four to thirty-six hours for the first assembly, and a further day for a final checking.

Félix had not appeared for lunch, and Hermann Kapp wondered what the woman did for food. This was his third job with her, and he had yet to see Félix eat anything at all. Why the devil, he wondered irritably, couldn't she be the same as other people.

A Chance for the Police

London, 7 A.M.

Willy Best had slept only fitfully on the overnight plane from Washington to London. He walked with a kind of otherworldly feeling from the plane along a corridor marked Arrivals. He walked on and on and on, until he came to feel he would soon be back in Washington again. At last the immigration desks appeared. Almost without pausing, he marched through British Passports Only. Since he had but a small hand case, he continued his march through the green customs area. But before reaching the exit he received a sharp command to stop. It had all been a bit too fast for the young sleepy-eyed customs official. Nobody, he felt, nobody innocent gets off a plane that quickly. The police identification which Willy Best showed him only served to heighten his suspicions. What an obvious ploy, he thought to himself, as he began to give this bloody obvious fake the going-over of a lifetime.

Willy Best thought about calling for the head customs officer, but then he reflected that the poor devil was probably just in the act of shaving, probably cutting himself too, somewhere over there in Hayes, Middlesex. Then

he thought about shouting for the airport manager, then
the Commissioner, then the Prime Minister. All these
natural impulses he sternly suppressed, for he had long
since learned that the quickest way to settle interdepart-
mental squabbles was never to let them happen. Yet by
the time he climbed wearily into a taxi, with the young
jack-in-office's surly apology still ringing in his ears, he
couldn't help noticing the difference between the way
it was in Britain and the way it had been in the United
States.

When he reached St. John's Wood it didn't help his
temper to find that nobody was around yet. To relieve
his mind, he began the day by writing a number of sharp
office memos. Then at 8:45 a messenger brought him a
sealed envelope. Best took one look at its contents and
shouted, "When did this come in?" The messenger said,
"Sometime during the night," and proceeded placidly
on his way, oblivious to the way things were, and oblivious
too to Willy Best's white-hot anger. For the envelope
contained the notes that Willy Best had himself made
in Washington on the previous day. Except that instead
of his own hastily scrawled pages it had all been neatly
set out and typed for him. In his anger and in his woefully
tired state he wondered how it could be that, if somebody
over there had taken all this trouble, then why couldn't
somebody over here have bothered themselves just to
make sure that the papers had been on his desk when
he'd arrived. People talked about the pace and pressure
of life being different, but Willy Best decided that such
talk was only a way of making excuses for laziness and
crass incompetence.

London, 17A Courtlane Mews, 7:30 A.M.

Al Simmonds had fitted himself up with a camp bed
down in the basement workshop, which had left a bed-

room each for Hermann Kapp, Abu l'Weifa, and Anna Morgue, while Sunion Webb occupied the quarters which the elderly caretakers usually reserved to themselves. It was typical of Simmonds that he liked to live right on top of the job, with the smell of lubricating oil in his nostrils. He had been up at five-thirty, raring to go. First he had brewed himself a pot of coffee and cooked himself a plate of bacon and eggs, followed by toast and marmalade. If the makings had been there, he would have done himself hash browns as well.

All through the previous day the others, especially Hermann Kapp, had talked and talked about the "design." They had made drawings, measuring it all up to the last fraction of a centimetre. Al Simmonds was glad of the drawings, of course, but he felt he didn't need them, really. The "design" would have grown in his mind as he went along. Everything would have come together, because he would have had all the measurements going ceaselessly round and round in his subconscious, and any contradictions among them would somehow have bubbled up to the surface. In brief, he would have been aware of anything that was going wrong. The drawings were fine, but they had cost nearly twenty-four hours. Kapp believed in drawings, because that was the way he had been taught at college. College, by Christ-on-a-donkey! The trouble with drawings was that they didn't tell you how long the job was going to take, how long it would take to set up the machines, how many hours for turning, for milling, drilling, fitting, for the thousand-and-one details the practical man had to cope with. For fellows like Kapp the "job" was an idea in the mind. For Al Simmonds the job was a matter of doing it, of making it a reality, and that was why he was now hard at it, moving easily backward and forward among the machines.

Someone had come down to the basement. Al Simmonds kept ostentatiously on with his work, just to emphasise his point. Then he noticed it was Félix, not Hermann or Pedro. What the hell did she want? The woman was just standing there, looking around for herself. Al Simmonds wondered why he didn't like this bitch. There weren't many women who couldn't give him a stand, but Félix was one of them all right. It was true he didn't like skinny types, but that wasn't all of it. And it wasn't her face, not her features anyway, because he wasn't too fussy, if the moment felt right. It wasn't just that the woman put the thought of frolics on the sofa out of his mind. She made him uneasy, so that he felt he might be slicing off his prick on one of the machines. He wished the bitch would get herself upstairs and stay there. Maybe he should tell her to go to bed with this old guy with the smoothed-back white hair, this Sunion Webb. Simmonds thought about Sunion Webb, and decided he didn't like him either.

London, Heathrow Airport, 11:45 A.M.

Dr. Ernest Carruthers had passed the immigration desk at building number 3. He had come quite early out to the airport, and he still had a good hour to wait until the Aeroflot flight to Moscow would be ready for boarding. He bought himself a cup of coffee at the snack bar, and took it away to one of the armchairs in the more distant part of the lounge. There he sat down to sip the coffee and read the newspaper he had also bought.

He had just finished the last of the coffee when he became aware of a man bearing down on him. The man asked if he might see his ticket. Thinking little of it, Ernest Carruthers immediately produced his ticket. Perhaps his flight had been delayed, which would be a nuisance, for

there would be friends waiting at Moscow Airport. Then
the man asked him to please come along, which Carruthers did without hesitation or unease. It wasn't until they
reached a corridor leading off the main lounge to a suite
of offices that Carruthers even troubled himself to ask
what the matter might be. He wondered a little that
there was no reply. He wondered more when he found
himself in one of the offices, confronted there by a slender
man with a sharp upright posture, a trim moustache, and
a full head of fair hair with a strong reddish tinge to it.
An obvious soldier type, Ernest Carruthers thought. He
stood over the man, leaning over him, and said in a now
testy voice, "Well, what is it?"

"We'd like to ask you a few questions."

"Who might I be speaking to?"

"Chief Inspector Robertson."

The man produced an identification card. So he was
police, not a soldier. Ernest Carruthers liked the police
even less than he liked the military, and since he was
not conscious of having done anything wrong, he allowed
his resentment and anger to grow rapidly. Nevertheless,
his reply was still fairly calm.

"Why do you wish to ask me questions, Inspector?"

"I'm afraid I can't tell you that, Dr. Carruthers."

"Perhaps you'd better let me hear the questions."

"When we get back into town," Cluny Robertson told
him.

It took a few seconds for the enormity of the situation
to become clear to Ernest Carruthers. Then the dam wall
broke within him.

"I am *not* going into town, either for you or anybody
else," he exclaimed.

"Oh yes, I'm afraid you are," was Robertson's imper-
turbable answer. Carruthers saw this upstart of a policeman standing there between himself and the office door.

With a sudden convulsive movement he pushed the fellow aside and launched himself toward the door.

Cluny Robertson knew nothing about why he had been asked to pick up this tall, crusty fellow. When he'd turned up for work that morning, Willy Best, all red and bleary in the face, and in the worst temper that Robertson could remember, had simply told him to locate the man. "Somewhere in the University," Best had shouted as he had rushed away to do something else. It had not taken long to check the complete University of London faculty list. From the list Cluny Robertson had found that Ernest Carruthers was on the staff of Imperial College. A call to the bursar's office at Imperial College had given him Carruthers' address, and a visit there established that Carruthers had gone out shortly before. Then Robertson had been lucky. A woman in a neighbouring apartment told him that Carruthers had only just left for the airport. Taking the chance that the airport would be Heathrow, Cluny Robertson had driven out of London along the M4 at top speed. Using the sirens at full blast, the young police constable who did the driving had in fact made the trip in twenty-five minutes flat, which had been some going in view of the state of the traffic. All Cluny Robertson knew about Carruthers to this point was that he was a very tall man—the woman in the neighbouring apartment had told him that—and the officer at the immigration desk had remembered it too. In fact, the immigration officer remembered enough of Carruthers to recognise him in the lounge. This was the way it had been up to the moment that Carruthers burst out of the office, pushing Robertson aside as he did so.

Cluny Robertson was a soldier now, not a policeman. With a snap at the immigration man "to fetch help," he was at Carruthers' heels. When the man tried to go through the exit to the departure gates, Robertson was ahead of him, curtly ordering two members of a waiting airline crew to give assistance. With the exit blocked, Carruthers simply stood there, shouting at him in blazing anger. Carruthers was in no mood to avoid a scene. In fact, a scene was exactly what he wanted, to show everybody what a lot of bloody Fascists were running the country. Three policemen appeared in the lounge, but even though he was now much outnumbered, Carruthers refused to "go quietly." He stood there, talking rapidly and angrily, with everybody in the lounge listening and watching. He stood high and tall, telling Cluny Robertson that he wasn't going anywhere. To which Robertson responded with the whiplash order, "March him." There was a short scuffle, and then Ernest Carruthers was propelled at some speed out of the lounge, out of the thronged concourse, to a police car. Because Carruthers continued to demonstrate even inside the car, it took considerably longer than twenty-five minutes to make the drive back to St. John's Wood. A true policeman would have deplored the scene back at the airport, but it never occurred to Robertson to worry in the least about it. Violence was his real business.

London, 17A Courtlane Mews, Noon

Al Simmonds, Abu l'Weifa, and Hermann Kapp were all hard at work. Simmonds had begun turning the outer cylinder, Abu l'Weifa was calculating the quantity of chemical explosive he would use, and Hermann Kapp was rapidly building up a circuit diagram. Kapp was pretty sure they were making the thing quite a bit heavier than it really needed to be. But he had wanted to make certain that the chemical explosive wouldn't blow the cylinder wall apart. So he had specified a tough, thick wall. Then, of course, all the other weights had been scaled up in proportion. The extra bulkiness had an advantage, however. Just as one can turn a refractory screw more readily with a heavy wrench than with a light one, so all the mechanics of the thing would work more smoothly in a heavy structure than in a light one. Hermann Kapp estimated the weight at about a ton, but the weight didn't really matter, because the job specification didn't call for the thing to be moved in any way. But a more solid job would take that bit longer to make. Yet even so, Hermann Kapp thought they would keep more or less on schedule.

Anna Morgue and Sunion Webb had gone out. Webb had been the first to leave, and he had been followed shortly thereafter by Anna Morgue, because following him was her job. Her job was to protect the flank of the operation, and Webb, not being one of "them," was a distinct part of the flank.

Sunion Webb took the underground from Gloucester Road to Piccadilly Circus. In the rotunda there he made several telephone calls. Then he booked another tube ticket, returning down the elevators to the Piccadilly Line, which he rode as far as Holborn. There he changed to the Central, going just one station, to Chancery Lane. From the Chancery Lane exit he walked to the Golden Cock Pub in Portpool Lane. He had often visited the Golden Cock during his London days, and he was glad to find the place not much changed from the way he remembered it. The two journalists he had contacted, first by telegram from Amsterdam, and now by phone from the Piccadilly Circus rotunda, were there already with a table booked in an upstairs room, away from the noise of the busy bar.

Sunion Webb was fully aware that this meeting in the Golden Cock was the most delicate part of his whole mission. But the world around him was his own world. Because of that he felt he could handle the situation. The big problem, of course, was to make the bomb threat credible. Simply telephoning the newspapers about it just would not have been sufficient. Anybody might do that. So perforce he had been obliged to declare himself. The two journalists he had contacted were acquaintances of long standing, both far-Left men, both with long records of hard-hitting, anti-establishment, antigovernment articles behind them, thorns in the flesh of the socialist centre, men unspeakable in conservative eyes, but thoroughly sound fellows in Sunion Webb's opinion. Jack Hart and Stan Tambling rose to greet him effusively as he came up the well-remembered flight of narrow creaking stairs. Old comrades in arms, they told themselves, as they each took a pull on their tankards of ale.

Sunion Webb had much of general interest to tell the reporters, but they knew that he would not have established contact with them merely to talk about interesting generalities. They also knew, as he did, that it would be good policy to wait until just 2 P.M., when most of their close neighbours at the surrounding tables would have left. The Golden Cock always cleared itself, as if by divine command, just after 2 P.M. So they were all happy to play along in avid reminiscence as they ate veal-and-ham pie and quaffed their first and second pints of ale.

The experienced reporter's natural instinct to protect his sources of information was Webb's first wall of defence. The wall he knew might eventually be forced to crack, but not soon enough to trouble him, he reckoned. It took many weeks or even months before official pressure on a journalist had any chance of forcing an unwilling disclosure. This would be a totally safe margin of time for Webb. By then he would be well clear of the country, the British veto would have been stopped, and in a small way he himself would have made a contribution to history.

The generalities were about Africa and about the possibility of the British veto, which had become a matter of open discussion over the past few days. Both Hart and Tambling had written stinging articles about the veto possibility, about what it would do to Britain's image throughout the world, about the callous indifference which it would imply to the aspirations of the Third World. The articles gave Sunion Webb some confidence that neither of the journalists would rush off and willingly reveal the source of the startling information which he would shortly be disclosing to them.

Anna Morgue was unhappy about the visit of Webb to the Golden Cock. She had managed to follow him through the to-and-fro on the underground system. The trail from Chancery Lane to Portpool Lane had been more straightforward. Anna Morgue went inside the pub herself and stood amongst the noisy crowd which surrounded the downstairs bar. She deduced correctly that Webb must have gone upstairs. She was especially unhappy because she felt there was an amateurish flavour about it all. Eventually as the crowd within the pub melted away, she went out into Portpool Lane and waited there until Webb emerged at about 2:45. There were two men with her quarry, and as she watched them strolling and gesticulating, she could tell by their gait that they had drunk far too much alcohol. This was a point of some severity with Anna Morgue, for she herself drank no alcohol at all.

Sunion Webb took the underground from Holborn back to Gloucester Road. His job was essentially finished now. Indeed, he saw no reason why he should emerge again from Courtlane Mews, not until the moment came for him to leave the country. By then he would be well clear of the riffraff that was now assembling the thing in the basement workshop. After glancing about the Mews for

a few seconds, he let himself into 17A. He went to the
elderly couple's room and then slumped in his shoes onto
the bed. He was conscious a few minutes later that one
of the others had come into the house. Beyond wondering
for a moment why anybody other than himself should
have reason to leave the house, he thought nothing more
of it.

Moscow, 4 P.M.

Within little more than an hour of the arrest of Ernest
Carruthers, the news of it was known in Moscow. There
was no mystery in how this came about. The steward
of the Aeroflot plane from Heathrow to Moscow had been
given particular instructions to make certain that Carruthers boarded the plane. When he did not do so, the
steward had done the natural thing—he had sought to
have an announcement for Carruthers made on the
Heathrow public address system. He had then been informed of the arrest by the switchboard operator, and
the news of it had simply been radioed to Moscow as
soon as the plane had quitted British territory.

Like a chess player suddenly faced with an unwelcome
move from his opponent, who then takes time over his
reply—even though the reply may be forced—Igor Markov had hesitated for a further hour before making his
response. The response had been to arrange for urgent
calls to be sent to the law firm of Stein, Stein, and Jung
in London, and to a lawyer in Stockholm with connexions
to Rights International, Inc.

London, St. John's Wood, 2:15 P.M.

Willy Best was feeling very tired. It was nearly thirty-
six hours since the Commissioner had dragged him out

of bed to make the trip to Washington. A lot of water had flowed under Westminster Bridge since then. He'd known from the moment this university fellow had been brought into his office that he wasn't going to get anywhere with him at all. Cluny Robertson had rubbed the man the wrong way, badly. It had been a mistake to send Cluny on that particular job. Forcing himself into the most winning smile that his swirling head and tired bones could muster, Willy Best had come straight out with it. What could Carruthers remember of the properties he had negotiated for the Anglo-Soviet Peace Association? By way of answer the man had simply laughed in his face.

In fact, Ernest Carruthers had been mighty glad to hear the question asked, so trivial did it seem to him. Even in his rage he had been combing around to think what it might be that the police were seeking. He had thought about minor tax irregularities. But as he had soon realised, it would hardly be a matter for the police to investigate those. So it came down to a piece of Right-wing harassment, just as he had instinctively supposed. And neither the police, nor any other Right-wing vermin, were going to get anything from him.

"He knows something, but he's not worried about it," Willy Best said to Cluny Robertson. Cluny was a bit miffed to find that his capture, over which he had been obliged to take considerable trouble, was only a shot in the dark. So Best explained about the CIA files, and about the list of Soviet-inspired agents he had found, and about those who were thought to be in the business of providing "safe" houses.

"The trouble," he concluded, "is that the Americans had some things wrong. Things I know are wrong. Maybe this is another mistake."

The phone rang, and Best picked up the receiver. He

did nearly all the listening, answering only in mono-
syllables.

"That," he said eventually and with a wry smile as
he replaced the receiver, "was Mr. David Kemp of Stein,
Stein, and Jung."

"Who might they be?"

"Lawyers. Gray's Inn."

"Wanting what?"

"You'd like to know, wouldn't you?" Willy Best grinned.
"You'd hardly believe it," he went on, "but Mr. David
Kemp was enquiring about Dr. Ernest Carruthers. Asked
if we were holding him."

"How would he know that?"

"The answer, Cluny my boy, could be very interesting.
Very interesting indeed. Or of course Mr. David Kemp
could simply have heard about your little affair out at
the airport. But very interesting, especially as he said
he was coming out here right away."

"He might be a close friend of Carruthers."

"Boyhood chums? Well, we shall be able to find out,
won't we?"

London, Fleet Street, 3 P.M.

Jack Hart and Stan Tambling wrote the articles which
conservatives found unspeakable in their content only
partly because of their own personal convictions. The
other part was that it paid them to write that way. The
newspaper for which they worked was supposed to have
inherited a great liberal tradition. But there was little
of old-style liberalism about the paper nowadays. In the
struggle for survival the paper had found it expedient
to move farther and farther to the Left, to appeal strongly
to the one-quarter of the British people who believed
the way Jack Hart and Stan Tambling wrote their articles.

The paper was strong on the South African situation. Scarcely a day passed without adverse comment on this situation appearing in its columns. Mostly the comment was routine stuff which also appeared in a more muted form in rival papers. From time to time, however, the paper launched itself into wholly new stories, alleging hitherto unreported enormities perpetrated by the South African government. But several of these stories had gone very sour in recent months, for the reason that they were demonstrably false, sheer fabrications of young men anxious to go one better than the truth itself. Jack Hart and Stan Tambling were both experienced reporters, however, not given to falling into such excesses. Their first thought, as they quickly sobered up from the pints of beer they had drunk at the Golden Cock, was that they were not going to put out a story that would immediately boomerang both on themselves and on their paper. So they made notes about the things Sunion Webb had told them, about things like the plutonium which the deceased Irish priest was supposed to have been carrying, and about the operation designed to prevent the British veto from being cast on the South African motion at the United Nations. Even as they wrote it all down it seemed a very tall story, and it was with misgivings that they went together to the Chief Editor's office to talk to him about it.

The Chief Editor's desk was rather small, not able to hold much in the way of piles of papers. He made up for this, however, by strewing papers all over the floor. On the evening of the last day of every month he had the whole office swept clean of its debris so as to begin the new month in a pristine condition. It now being the 16th of August, the place was already beginning to assume its end-of-the-month pigsty appearance. The Chief Editor was a small man who nevertheless contrived to look like a big frog. He always sniffed whenever a reporter brought him copy to read, and he sniffed loudly all the time now as he read the notes which Jack Hart and Stan Tambling had brought. Like a bloody great frog of a dog, Jack Hart thought to himself.

The Chief Editor paused in his reading and the sniffing came to an abrupt stop. He stabbed at one of the sheets with a short thick finger. "You've got it! Here!" he exclaimed. "It says they brought a car through Harwich to the railway station at Colchester. Find that car and find the stuff on it and we'll go in with all guns firing!" he shouted, throwing the notes back at the two reporters.

Outside the Chief Editor's office they tossed a coin to decide who should go to Colchester and who should stay behind to write the first draft of the story. Jack Hart won the toss and decided to make the trip to Colchester.

London, St. John's Wood, 3 P.M.

David Kemp was a well-proportioned young man with a quick, firm step. His fair hair, while thick, lay flat on his head and it was neatly brushed at the temples and at the back. His face was rather round and of a high colour. His voice had plenty of volume with bass resonances in it, and his speech showed no trace of any indigenous accent. He was shown by a plainclothes detective constable into Willy Best's room. Best rose from his chair, managing what he hoped was his most friendly manner. "Ah, Mr. Kemp. You're right on time, Sir. This is Chief Inspector Robertson, who made the arrest earlier today."

Willy Best was fascinated to notice that Kemp was wearing a suit and waistcoat, even on a warm August afternoon, and in the waistcoat he was sporting an old-fashioned watch and chain, with which he now fiddled as he turned to Cluny Robertson.

"Ah, quite a deplorable scene I understand."

"I didn't find it deplorable . . . ," Cluny began, and then caught the sign-off look in Willy Best's eye.

"It won't sound good in court," Kemp added.

"No. Well, we'll worry about that when we come to it," Best interposed in his most affable tenor voice. "What would you be here for, Mr. Kemp, might I ask?"

"To see my client, of course." Kemp's voice was loud, clear, and plum-rich in quality.

"I don't know we have any client of yours," Best countered.

"Come now, Superintendent, I'm talking about Dr. Ernest Carruthers. Carruthers is an old client of my firm."

"I don't know anything about his being an old client of your firm, Mr. Kemp."

"You can take my word for it."

Willy Best began pencil twiddling with his right hand. Robertson had seen him do it with the left hand, but mostly it was the right hand.

"Come now, Mr. Kemp, you must know it isn't my business to take people's word for this kind of thing. Before I consider letting you see Carruthers, I want myself to see a letter of instruction from him to your firm. It's Stein, Stein, and Jung, isn't it?"

"May I use your phone?" David Kemp asked in a now angry voice.

"By all means."

The young lawyer stabbed out a city number on the dial. Best heard the click of a receiver being lifted at the other end. "Is that Mr. Hardcastle? Mr. Hardcastle, I want the file on Dr. Ernest Carruthers sent immediately. Yes, out to the Police Special Branch. Yes, in St. John's Wood. Just as fast as you can." David Kemp slammed the phone down, and went on, "And now I'd like to see my client."

"Very good, Mr. Kemp, very well done." Willy Best

was back at his pencil twiddling. "We'll take a look at the file when it arrives," he added.

"You're simply wasting time, Superintendent."

"Oh no, I don't think so. I'll tell you what, Mr. Kemp. We'll study the file overnight. If we think it's in order, we'll give you a call at Stein, Stein, and Jung tomorrow morning. Then you may come out here again, tomorrow afternoon, twenty-four hours from now, and we will discuss your seeing the prisoner." Best's voice was calm and matter-of-fact.

David Kemp picked up the case he had deposited on the floor a few minutes earlier. "You're going to be very sorry about this, Superintendent," he said tersely, in a low, controlled voice.

"It was a good try, Mr. Kemp, but just a little bit too thin."

David Kemp moved swiftly to the door. As he went out, Best called after him, "And try to remember to take along the right file the next time you're sent out on a job."

When the young lawyer had gone, Best continued to Cluny Robertson, "He'd have done better to have waited."

"For what?"

"For his office to have had time to fake that file."

"You're certain it will be a fake?"

"Certain of it. You know, I'm beginning to have a sort of feeling about your prisoner."

"What feeling, man?"

"I think I'm going to have a talk to Barry Gwent about Carruthers. We're much too nice to be handling this sort of case. Being an army man yourself, you'll know what I mean." Best had stopped his pencil twiddling, the affable look had gone from his face, his grey eyes had clouded, and there was a threat both in his voice and in the manner in which he now rose from his chair.

Colchester, Essex, 5:40 P.M.

Jack Hart, accompanied by a young fellow from the newspaper's transport department, alighted from the London train. His first move, after winning the toss from Stan Tambling, had been to go to the transport department, to find somebody there who knew the trick of opening locked cars and of starting cars without an ignition key. The two of them had gone to Liverpool Street station and had caught one of the business-hour trains to Colchester. By 5:40 they had located the railway parking lot. In fact, they simply tagged along with other passengers who were walking to their cars.

There were enough people walking about the parking lot to give them plenty of time to study the lines of cars without any fear of being noticed. And indeed it took them quite a while to find Klaus Hartstein's abandoned VW, because the parking lot had a fair sprinkling of foreign cars in it. There was a slip of paper under the VW's wiper, demanding two days' extra payment for parking. Jack Hart grinned at this ridiculous detail, and then thought it might be good policy to pay off the demand. His young colleague had the VW open in astonishingly little time, so little that Jack Hart wondered why buyers troubled themselves to pay for the locks on their car doors. A moment or two later the young fellow also had the engine started and they began easing their way into a line of cars which was moving slowly toward the exit from the lot.

London, St. John's Wood, 7:30 P.M.

Willy Best waited alone in his room. He had put through a call to Barry Gwent, although it had been against his policeman's instinct to use the phone. It wasn't that he was worried about security because he had access

to a special line. It was rather that policemen like to
see people's faces, not like civil servants who use the
phone all the time and who are not interested in people's
faces.

To Best's surprise, Barry Gwent had said he would
come immediately into London himself, and a meeting
had been set up for 7:30. At that precise time there was
a loud knock on the door. Best jumped quickly from his
chair, although by now his legs and back were aching
badly from all the travelling and sitting and the lack of
sleep. And his stomach was beginning to act up more
than a bit from the ragbag assortment of food he had
thrown into it at various odd moments over the past forty
hours.

To Willy Best's further surprise, Gwent was not alone.
He was accompanied by an older man, a short, slender man with silvery white hair and a small dark moustache.

"General Holland," Gwent introduced, and Willy Best
managed to dredge a last welcoming smile from his weary
self as he shook the offered hand.

"Glad to meet you, General Holland," he nodded.

"Gwent has been telling me about your problem," Holland began, immediately assuming command.

"It's good of you to come, Sir."

"Not good at all. It's my duty, Superintendent. You're
sure about this man, this Carruthers?"

"I'm sure he knows something. I'm not sure what or
how much."

"I need to know how sure is 'sure.' If you can see what
I mean."

"It's been growing strongly on me through the afternoon. Just after six this evening we had a call from the
immigration people at Heathrow."

"Yes?"

"To say they'd noticed a Rights International, Inc., lawyer. Came in on a plane from Sweden."

"No proof in that."

"My betting is that by tomorrow morning we'll be having an approach to the Home Secretary."

"From this lawyer?"

"Yes. You might like to have his name." Best picked up a slip of paper and handed it to General Holland.

"Paco Palmgren," Holland read out. "Mean anything to you?" he asked Gwent.

"Yes, Sir. We saw a lot of him when the northern Ireland enquiry was going on," Gwent replied immediately. "Better keep your eye on him, Super, he's a slippery bastard."

"I put a man on him right away," Best told them, hoping within himself that Cluny Robertson would manage not to make another uproar out of it.

"I'll be frank with you, Superintendent, I can't do anything without the Home Secretary's consent," Holland continued.

"I doubt you'll get that. Not soon enough, at any rate."

"In view of your assurances, Superintendent, I'm going to approach Henry Fielding myself, this evening. I can't offer fairer than that."

Holland was right, of course. Willy Best knew that Military Intelligence was carrying a load of shell eggs on its back, at any rate so far as interrogations were concerned. The European Court on Human Rights had the British government by the short hairs, and the government had MI by the short hairs. The damnable thing about it was it wouldn't take more than an hour or two for MI to make this Carruthers cough up everything he knew. Willy Best would have taken a bet that inside himself Carruthers was a soft type.

London, Fleet Street, 8:15 P.M.

A mechanic in the transport department had been
asked to stay on after normal working hours. He had
the VW lifted up on a big hydraulic jack and he was
examining the fittings of the petrol tank.

"I'd say it's been off recently," he told Jack Hart, the
Chief Editor, and Stan Tambling. "But it's got a lot of
muck on it," he added.

It took an irritatingly long time to get the tank off,
particularly as it was heavy with more than sixty pounds'
weight of petrol slopping about inside it. They all helped
to support the damned tank as the mechanic released
the last of its fastenings. It was a relief when they had
it turned over and had emptied the petrol into two cans.
Then the mechanic put the tank on a bench and began
to scrape away the dirt from the bottom. There was a
moment of thrill as the mud came away. There, set in
a waxy material, four screw heads could be seen. The
mechanic had the flat-ended screw out in a minute or
two more. Then he reached inside the false bottom of
the tank and removed from it one of the two flat objects
which the pilot Luri Otto had brought to the Schönefelt
Airport of East Berlin. The mechanic immediately pulled
the dun-coloured wrapping off the object to reveal what
looked only like a flat lump of lead. He rubbed the thing
down, saying, "Looks like lead, only the bloody thing's
hot."

The three others suppressed their inclination to whoop
it up. They all realised that it was best to say nothing
in front of the mechanic. True, the mechanic would be
curious about the VW and about the hot piece of lead,
but any man working for a newspaper expects curious
things to happen.

The Chief Editor took the leadlike object to his office.

Jack Hart and Stan Tambling followed him, taking care to shut the outer door.

"It's the story of the century, boys," the Chief Editor shouted. "Front page spread, whole front page. Get it finished fast."

"How about this thing?" asked Stan Tambling, pointing to the leadlike object.

"I've thought about that," the Chief Editor nodded. "It would be nice in a way to hold it back. Just to have 'em denying everything. I can just hear 'em denying it. Then we could go even bigger with this baby." The Chief Editor picked the object up again. "Bloody heavy thing," he interjected, "too heavy for it all to be lead. And if it was, it couldn't be hot, could it. Not any lead that I know about. Well, it would be nice to have 'em on the hook, wouldn't it, damned bloody nice. But there's just the possibility . . ." The Chief Editor paused for a moment, holding up a short finger, ". . . it's just possible they might slap a D notice on us. Then we'd lose it. So what I say is go ahead. With the lot, photographs and all. Get to work, boys."

Just as inveterate photographers continue to run their cameras even in the face of an exploding volcano, so Jack Hart and Stan Tambling erupted out of the Chief Editor's office. The prospect of an enormous scoop filled their minds. It was the ultimate moment for which they had waited over more than twenty years, over most of their working lives.

London, Albany, 9:45 P.M.

Henry Fielding was giving a small dinner party in his rooms in Albany, a party for two industrialists and their wives, two industrialists who might be useful to him should the "party" ever find itself in opposition. In the wilderness, as Henry Fielding always thought of it. During the entrée he had been interrupted by his PPS. The young man had come to him with two messages, one from Holland of MI, the other from Rights International, Inc. The juxtaposition was ominous, and the Home Secretary had struggled in vain to dismiss it from his mind during the dessert. The moment came at last for the ladies to powder themselves, and for the men to peedle-weedle, and in this moment Henry Fielding escaped for a while to find out what Holland had on his mind.

The General had been waiting there in a small office for forty-five minutes, and the waiting had not improved his temper. In terse phrases with nothing to spare he described Willy Best's problem. The Home Secretary smoothed his long straight hair over the high crown of his head.

"No," he said immediately, as soon as Holland had finished. "This is a police matter. Let them do the job. I'm not having them push it off onto MI."

"He can't do the job. He's not allowed to," said Holland in a sharp, clipped way.

"And neither are you," the Home Secretary replied in a similar tone.

As he walked out of Albany, through its locked gate into Piccadilly, General Holland knew he had done what he could, and it was not much, In fact, it was nothing at all. As he walked toward Hyde Park Corner he felt more hot, subdued anger than he had in years. Not good at his age, the doctors would tell him. As he neared Hyde Park Corner he found himself turning over in his mind whether there was really nothing more that he could do.

A Matter of Timing

London, 17A Courtlane Mews, 1 A.M.

Hermann Kapp had called a halt to the work at 11:30 P.M. on the 16th. The construction had gone on all through the 16th, and by 11:30 it was nearing completion. At least in Hermann Kapp's mind it was nearing completion, if not in the opinion of Al Simmonds. Simmonds would have gone endlessly on, rechecking and refining to tolerances far above what was needed. It was indeed to put a stop to this potentially endless fussing that Kapp had called the end to the day's activities. Already the thing was better made than was really necessary. Any old bringing together of the two pieces of uranium would do, so long as the release of the neutron source was properly timed. And as he had thought more about it, Kapp had realized that the simplest fracture of the foil separating the boron from the α-active material would be sufficient. This he had seen was certain to happen, even if the foil was not melted or vaporized. The merest generation of neutrons at precisely the right moment would be sufficient for the thing to go sky-high, literally. So with the job essentially completed, apart from the final systems check, he had sent everybody packing off to bed.

But even by 1 A.M. nobody at 17A Courtlane Mews was asleep. Kapp himself was not disturbed by anything really complex. Yet the thought of what they had done was itself sufficient to make him wakeful. The little half-pint radical who thought he was organising everything, this quaint Sunion Webb, had told him about the arranged exit route. That was fixed for the morning of the 18th, which gave more than ample time for the systems check. Then the job would be done, and the second part of the payment of two million Swiss francs would be made. Or would it? This question also kept him wakeful.

Al Simmonds was sleeping only a few yards away from the thing. Little Boy, they had called the first one at Los Alamos. In a way this too was the first of its kind. The thought of lying so close to it didn't disturb Simmonds at all. He was more disturbed by the way his mind kept going over and over all the practical details of its construction. He kept wondering whether it mightn't have been better to do this or that bit of the job in a somewhat different way. Other possible designs kept thrusting themselves into the front of his mind. Then the really troublesome question began to worry him. Were the four of them getting a fair price for the job?

Two million Swiss francs, Hermann Kapp had told him. Half a million apiece to each of the four of them, although Simmonds couldn't see what the bitch of a woman was doing to deserve a share. That would be about two hundred thousand dollars for his own share. Which wasn't hay. Pretty good by any standards. But even so, was it enough? Wouldn't the British pay a lot more just to be rid of the thing? To Simmonds the potential blackmail suddenly seemed enormous. They were simply giving the job away, he decided as he tossed fitfully on his narrow camp bed.

Sunion Webb now found himself with most of his worries gone. To inform the press it had been necessary to expose himself. He'd known it would be so from the beginning. Was it only five, or was it six, days since he'd been in Moscow? So much had happened and so much had been successfully accomplished. Merely contemplating it all kept him awake, more or less pleasurably so.

Abu l'Weifa was a long way ahead of Al Simmonds in his thinking. Usually he worked under vastly more difficult conditions than the relatively ideal situation downstairs in the basement workshop. Usually he worked under conditions that were physically and materially difficult, often with very little time to spare. The recent job in Madrid had been a cliff-hanger of an affair involving hairline timing, down to the very last second.

Through the early part of the day he had worked with his normal acute sense of urgency, so that by the early evening he had approached the end of his part of the job. He'd spent the ensuing hours ostensibly watching the others. But deep in his mind his thoughts has been far away from the basement workshop, far away from London itself. He'd remembered his friends rotting in Spanish jails, and the concept had germinated within him that this thing they were assembling had the most enormous leverage on the British government. Not for money but for political pressure. Political pressure from London to the Common Market in Brussels, to Madrid. The details of how the leverage might be exercised needed careful working out. But the main idea was there and it seemed eminently sound. Abu l'Weifa turned the matter over and over, and still he could see nothing wrong with it, except perhaps the involvement of Mr. Sunion Webb. Abu l'Weifa chuckled quietly to himself in the darkness of the night.

The thoughts of Anna Morgue were the most complex

of the five new residents of 17A Courtlane Mews. Her thoughts were of power. Power over people and power over the march of events. As a girl she had been fascinated by history. She had then read widely and voraciously, swallowing historical details from all periods indiscriminately. At college, however, she had gradually limited herself to medieval studies because it had been in medieval times that personal power had risen to its greatest height. The margin between ruler and ruled had then attained its greatest dimension, greater than at any other time in human history. It was an age in which there had been no escape for the dissident, an age in which the rebel could be mercilessly hunted down, imprisoned in an impregnable castle, and then destroyed physically and mentally, either quickly or very slowly at the ruler's pleasure. Many of the rulers, Anna Morgue noticed, had been women. There had been more women of great power in those days than at any time since. True power, not the pallid stuff of the present-day political world.

Explosives used in firearms and cannon had at last destroyed the medieval world. So Anna Morgue had come to see power in firearms and explosives. For it was surely a case, she reasoned, of a greater form of physical power replacing a lesser form. Her great natural talent in the use of firearms had quickly become apparent, aiding the evolution of her thoughts and of her personality. She saw herself as inheriting the compulsive strength of the medieval age. Nothing which had elapsed in the few years since she had arrived at this conclusion had done anything but persuade her of its truth.

The thing downstairs was of a certainty the ultimate explosive. Therefore in the logic of Anna Morgue's thinking, it must represent the quintessence of raw physical power. But how to make use of it in a personal way? There was the problem, the problem which now occupied the mind of Anna Morgue. Unlike most other terrorists she had no taste for frightening people she could not see. Abstract terror had no meaning for her. It was the direct power of the medieval castle that she craved, and it was this which she now intended to seek.

London, Fleet Street, 3 A.M.

Jack Hart and Stan Tambling had waited around for the London edition of their paper to come off the press. Unfortunately their blazing story had been written too late to meet the deadline for the provincial edition. This was a pity but not a catastrophe. Like everybody else centred on London, Jack Hart and Stan Tambling thought of the provinces as distant places, desirable places in a way, but not really to be considered seriously as places in which a reasonable man might live. And both reporters had more than half a suspicion that outside the environs of London their story would not have quite its full arresting quality. There might even be a sort of perverse welcome for it, connected in a way with all the endless chatter about devolution. It wasn't so much that the Scots wanted Scotland for the Scots, or the Welsh wanted Wales for the Welsh, Cornwall for the Cornish, Cumbria for the Cumbrians. It was more that everybody outside London was heartily sick of London, and quite a lot of people might start hugging themselves at the thought of London being blown to perdition.

The Chief Editor had long since gone home. In fact, he'd gone home to bed just as soon as he had finished the long editorial which now straddled the leader page. The Chief Editor had long since learned to relax, and that was exactly why he was Chief Editor.

Hart and Tambling made their weary way from the newsroom to the nearby parking lot where they habitu-

ally deposited their old runabouts during daylight hours—
there was no percentage in trying to drive around day-
time London. Both knew, as the engines of their respec-
tive cars wheezed and clattered into life, that the London
edition was even now being carried in vans hither and
thither over the metropolitan area. It was being carried
in stacks a foot thick with wrappers around them. Nobody
handling the stacks would know anything about that shattering front page, with its photographs of the VW, the
petrol tank, and the hot-lead thing. Or about the political
aspects of it all. Just as on any other day, the stacks would
be thrown out of the vans at various distributing points,
and they would remain there as uninformative stacks until around six o'clock when paper sellers all over the city
began to slit them open.

Here and there copies would be specially delivered,
however, and these would be examined sooner. At the
BBC, all the morning newspapers would be examined
in time for the early news bulletin. And if Stan Tambling
and Jack Hart had troubled themselves to think about
it they would have realised that special copies would be
examined even before that, by Reuters and by Associated
Press. The story would be around the world long before
the London paper sellers arrived on the job. Neither of
the reporters thought about this almost instantaneous
spread of their story, or about the phones that would
soon be disturbing the sleep of the most prominent persons in the land.

Both Hart and Tambling, as they drove to their separate homes, were much occupied in assessing their personal positions. The spot they were in was unquestionably
hot. There would be insistent pressure on them to reveal
the source of their information. Both found themselves
wondering how far the ethics of their profession ex-

tended. Both found themselves thinking about Sunion Webb.

London, Albany, 4 A.M.

The phone rang in Henry Fielding's bedroom. It had been fitted with the more discreet type of bell, the kind which sounds like the chirrup of an irritating and persistent bird. Aware that he had a slight hangover from the wine of the previous evening, but unaware of the events which had led to the call, the Home Secretary reached out vaguely to where the phone stood in its cradle upon a bedside table.

Because of the five hours' time difference between Western Europe and Washington, Hart and Tambling's story had already reached a presidential aide by 11 on the previous evening. The aide had deliberated whether to call the President himself about it, knowing that the President would be relaxing with a last cigar and a mystery novel before sleeping. The aide had decided to make the call, and the President, after thinking for a few minutes, had put through a call of his own to Heisal Woods. The Secretary of State had also thought about it for a few minutes and had then called the President back with the opinion that the story might conceivably have some substance in it. Secretary Woods had gone on to say that it would be his advice to call the British Prime Minister right away. This the President had done immediately. The British Prime Minister clearly knew nothing about the story, which helped persuade the President that it was only a media figment. Although the Prime Minister had been his usual affable self, after a few further minutes there had seemed little point in continuing the conversation. So the President had returned to his mystery novel, and the Prime Minister had called the Home Secretary.

The Prime Minister, after mentioning the newspaper story, wanted to know what was going on, and the Home Secretary, smoothing his hair over the crown of his head, said that so far as he knew nothing was going on. At that, the Prime Minister had told him to get up off his bloody arse and start moving. So the Home Secretary called his PPS and told him to contact the office's chief press agent. Henry Fielding stressed that it was vital for a denial of the story to reach the BBC before the first of the morning news bulletins went out. He also instructed his PPS to set up a top-level meeting for 9 A.M. sharp. With this done he climbed thankfully back into bed. He lay there for a while and then went to the bathroom where he relieved himself and took a couple of aspirins.

London, St. John's Wood, 6 A.M.

Willy Best had been exceedingly sluggish in getting himself out of bed, following still another early morning call from the Commissioner. He had been very deep under when the call came through at about 5 A.M. He had spent time brewing himself a pot of tea in spite of the urgency of the situation, hoping the tea would quieten the sickness in his stomach. Then he had driven shakily to his office, to find Sir Stanley Farrar there already with copies of all the morning dailies.

"It's only in this bloody one," the Commissioner began. Best took the offered paper. The front page certainly left little to the imagination.

"The editorial is worse," the Commissioner went on.

The editor wanted to know how it came about that neither the police nor the government itself were aware of facts vital to the national security, facts which his newspaper had been able to discover for itself.

"A good question," Best grunted. "I'd like to know the answer to that one myself."

"Perhaps we'll get an answer."

"Only if the bloody paper wants to tell us."

"There won't be any holds barred on this one," the Commissioner said grimly.

Willy Best put the paper down. "I wouldn't set much store by it. What will it come down to in the end, after a lot of legal argy-bargy? A phone call, maybe, a tip-off to some reporter. There won't be anything solid to it."

He reached over his desk, flicking the switch of a radio, just in time to hear the six o'clock pips. There it all was, now for the whole nation to hear. Following the story itself, the announcer read out a bland denial from a Home Office "spokesman."

"Bloody fools," grunted Best as he switched off the radio.

"Denying it can't do much harm," the Commissioner said in a milder voice than he felt. It was on the point of Willy Best's tongue to say that denying the story couldn't do much good either when the essential irrelevancy of it struck him.

"You know, Sir, it could be a rather clever trick. To put us off the real scent."

"This fellow Carruthers."

"Yes, Sir. I've got it winding around inside me all the time, that Carruthers is our one real lead."

"I've got a man from Rights International, Inc., coming to see me this morning. About Carruthers."

"Palmgren?"

"That's the name. You know him?"

"The immigration people told me. Yesterday evening. I should have called you about it."

"I'd have been glad, not knowing about him. But Field-

ing insists on my seeing the man. I'll try to keep you
out of it."

Willy Best decided this was the moment to mention
his meeting with General Holland and Barry Gwent.

"I contacted MI about Carruthers, Sir. It seemed a reasonable thing to do, after the way they handled the plutonium analysis for us."

"I know about that too. General Holland phoned."

Sir Stanley Farrar had a grim look set across his face,
which Best at first thought might be directed against
himself.

"Holland would like to do something for us, about Carruthers. But his hands are tied," Sir Stanley added.

"They'll be tied even more by this Palmgren fellow."

"Not if I can help it."

Willy Best looked down at the papers on his desk, moving them about a bit. He would have liked the Commissioner to continue, but the least said the better. Time
was the trouble. It was slipping away and nothing was
being done. By rights he himself should be doing something effective instead of shuffling bits of paper around
aimlessly on his desk. Willy Best felt as if he were being
suffocated in a forest of cotton wool.

London, 17A Courtlane Mews, 8 A.M.

Al Simmonds had woken somewhat later than usual,
about 6:30. As on the previous day, he had gone upstairs
to make himself a pot of coffee and to cook himself the
kind of solid breakfast he liked to start the day with.
While he was at work with the frying pan he heard someone come into the house. Sunion Webb had come quite
silently up the stairs from the street door with a bundle
of newspapers under his arm. Simmonds had noticed
Webb without being noticed himself. He had thought

nothing of it, until a few minutes later when he had switched on the kitchen radio. The 7 A.M. news began just as he was lifting fried eggs from the pan onto a plate.

One of the eggs slipped away from the spoon he was using. It missed the plate and even the table, shattering itself on the kitchen floor. Simmonds scarcely noticed the unsightly daub. Slamming down the frying pan, he was in on Sunion Webb in a matter of seconds. Without apology he grabbed hold of the papers, scanning them until he came to the one with the news. With mixed feelings he read quickly down the strident front page. Then he calmed down quickly, just as quickly as the excitement had burst on him only a few moments before. He calmed down because he thought the article a bum lead. Unless the Brits knew a lot more than this it would get them nowhere fast. In fact, there was a good part to the story. It went to confirm mightily the thoughts he'd been thinking during the night. The thing downstairs was big, real big, and Al Simmonds was more than ever convinced they were letting it go for peanuts.

Then he stalked into Hermann Kapp's room. The German too became excited as he read the news report. He didn't like the way it stared at him in huge black letters. He didn't like any of it, and unlike Simmonds, he didn't calm down at all. He dressed himself rapidly, telling Simmonds to rout out the others, but to keep out of his way for a while. Then he went into the housekeeper's room to discuss the situation with Sunion Webb.

Hermann Kapp voiced his objections in clear, cogent terms. He was excited, as his rapid speech showed, but the logic of his point of view did not falter. He had estimated one and a half days for assembly together with a further day for checking. Which amounted to sixty hours, he pointed out, sixty hours that would not be up until the late evening of that same day, the 17th. This story in the newspaper, he said, should have been postponed for one further day. Was this not the way it had been agreed?

Sunion Webb saw there was no sense in attempting to deny his own connexion with the newspaper story. So he pointed out that by tomorrow it would all have been too late, because tomorrow was the day of the Security Council debate. *"But that should have been said before,"* Kapp shouted indignantly. Webb thought the German's misgivings entirely misplaced, and he said so. There was nothing in the newspaper story to give the slightest clue to their whereabouts. So what was the fuss about?

The fuss, Kapp told him, was that the airports would very likely be closed. What airline would fly its planes into Britain in the face of this kind of threat? There would be a very much tighter surveillance at every exit point from the country. His plans had called for all four of them to be away by midnight, away with at least six hours to spare. Did Webb take him for a fool?

Sunion Webb remained calm. He wasn't taking anybody for a fool, he said. He reminded Kapp that an exit route had already been arranged. He took an envelope from a sideboard and showed its contents to the German. Kapp studied the several sheets of paper briefly and then nodded in a somewhat mollified way. He would discuss it with the others, he told Webb. Which he did, immediately. He assembled the others in the basement workshop. He told them of the exit which had been arranged, and he showed them the sheets of paper which Webb had handed to him.

But exit route or not, Hermann Kapp had no intention of depending anymore on Webb. Once bitten, he would be very shy from now on. Thoughts of leaving 17A Court-lane Mews were crowding the front of his mind, and a means of leaving better than his own two feet was plainly needed. He checked that Al Simmonds had a valid U.S. driver's license, and then told him to go out to hire a vehicle. Kapp saw no difficulty when Pedro said that he too would like to go along for the ride. Pedro said he was in need of air, and Hermann Kapp felt a bit the same way. But he himself still had a few hours' work to do on the "thing." Kapp was both careful and thorough, which was exactly why he was in charge of this operation, and exactly why he had always kept himself out of trouble.

London, St. John's Wood, 8:30 A.M.

Ernest Carruthers was brought up to Willy Best's room for the third time since he had been arrested on the previous day. During the long waiting periods in the cell, when he'd had plenty of time to cool off, he'd found himself wondering if it wouldn't be simplest to tell the police what they wanted to know. He'd been over in his mind all his dealings with the Anglo-Soviet Peace Association. There wasn't a great deal of it to tell. He could soon have got it off his chest, much good might it do them. But on each of the two previous occasions when he'd been brought out from his cell the enormity of what was being done to him had obliterated all such thoughts of easy compromise. Why should he allow himself to be bullied in this way? As Carruthers saw it, he had rights as an Englishman which the police and the bourgeois government would dearly love to suppress. In the moments when he was out of the cell, he'd seen it as his bounden duty to stand up for his rights. They couldn't keep him there indefinitely, he reasoned. His friends would start asking about him. Sooner or later they must allow him a lawyer, and when they did the boot would very definitely be on the other foot.

Carruthers stood to his full height of six feet five inches on the carpet in Willy Best's room. His long arms were tensed and his neck and head were slightly thrust forward. Once again he didn't like the way the policeman kept on sitting there, twiddling a pencil in his right hand.

"I hope you've thought better of it overnight, Dr. Carruthers. I mean about the simple question I've been asking you," Best began, quite unaware of the irritant effect of the pencil. He would have liked to add that the question wouldn't carry much of a penalty. But he was explicitly debarred by police rules from offering any such implied bargain. It all had to come out first, before there could be any question of waiving a charge against a prisoner, not like the American plea-bargaining system. Besides, it wasn't fear of prosecution that was holding Carruthers back. It was obstinacy and a detestation of the whole British establishment.

Carruthers spread out his tensed arms.

"This," he said indicating his own condition, "has to come to an end sometime. So you might just as well end it now. You can't hold me without a charge indefinitely, and when you charge me I shall ask for a lawyer."

"Do you have a lawyer in mind?"

"I have several."

Willy Best turned over a newspaper so that Carruthers could see the garish headlines on the front page.

"Read it," he said.

Carruthers took the paper and quickly ran through the article which Jack Hart and Stan Tambling had composed the previous evening.

"Well?" he asked in some puzzlement when he had done.

"You don't know anything about it?"

"Obviously not. It's a typical piece of scare journalism."

"If I told you that it might not be a scare at all, if I told you that the question I've been asking you has a direct connexion with it, if I appealed to you as an Englishman to answer that question, what would you say, Dr. Carruthers?"

There was an expression of blank incredulity on Carruthers' face. During the few seconds which the vacant look took to clear away, Best thought there was a chance he might win. Then he saw Carruthers do the double-think trick and the chance was gone.

"I wouldn't believe you. I wouldn't believe you, because it would be ridiculous," Carruthers replied.

Willy Best smiled as genuinely as he could manage.

"It isn't ridiculous, Dr. Carruthers. It's the truth. Don't try to be always looking for second meanings in what I say. Take it simply at its face value."

"Your life would be easy if everybody did that, wouldn't it, Superintendent?"

Willy Best managed to keep on smiling.

"It would help," he admitted.

"Are you asking me to believe that the Soviet Union is involved in terrorist activities?"

"Yes, that's what I'm asking you to believe, Dr. Carruthers."

"Have you ever been to the Soviet Union, Superintendent?"

Best shook his head.

"Or read very much about the Soviet Union?" Carruthers went on, with the edge of anger now in his voice.

Willy Best continued shaking his head.

"Then don't talk such rubbish," Carruthers concluded.

With a sigh, Willy Best saw that he had failed yet again. The man was just programmed the wrong way. Black was white, and white was black, blue was orange, and orange was blue. Short of weeks of wearisome argument

there was no unhooking the situation, not by any methods
which he himself could use.

London, Scotland Yard, 10:30 A.M.

Sir Stanley Farrar stormed up to his office, where Paco
Palmgren was waiting for him. It wasn't the thought of
the Swede that was making Sir Stanley angry. In fact,
he'd quite forgotten that on the previous day his secretary
had arranged for him to meet Palmgren there at ten
o'clock. It was the nine o'clock meeting at the Home
Office which had made him see red. The calm presump-
tion of the Home Secretary, abetted by his senior civil
servants, that the police should have known about this
damned newspaper story. The difficulty facing the Commissioner was to make them understand the enormity
of what was happening, the international ramifications
of it all. The Home Secretary and his people just couldn't
conceive that they themselves were really very small min-
nows in a pond which contained some very big fish indeed. Short of telling it plainly to the man, straight in
his face, there seemed no way to make him understand.
The Home Secretary's defect, Sir Stanley thought grump-
ily, came from attending in his impressionable years one
of the older universities.

Paco Palmgren was a well-built man in his middle for-
ties. He was a skiing enthusiast who kept himself in excellent condition. He was carefully but plainly dressed, except for the tie which had a slightly extravagant flair
about it. His head was large, but it was well carried on
a firm neck and shoulders. A cartoonist would have emphasised the length of the head, the rather large nose,
the wide-set eyes, and the slightly splayed angle of the
highly polished shoes. The Commissioner knew as soon
as he set eyes on Palmgren that the man's courtesy would
be impeccable.

"Thank you for seeing me, Sir Stanley," Palmgren began, implying that the half hour he had been kept waiting was of no consequence.

"I'm sorry I'm late," the Commissioner felt he must say.

"So am I, Sir Stanley. But not for myself. For a Dr. Carruthers, whom I am here to discuss with you."

"Why are you here, Mr. Palmgren?"

"To make sure that this man is properly treated. I am not here to argue whether he is innocent or guilty of some crime. That is for your law courts to decide."

"Mr. Palmgren, this man, as you call him, has been under arrest for less than twenty-four hours. It is surely curious for you to be enquiring about him so quickly. Do I make my point clear?"

"Absolutely clear, Sir Stanley. The first thing in answer to your question is that my organization, Rights International, Inc., was asked to investigate the circumstances of the arrest of Dr. Carruthers."

"By whom?"

"It is not necessary that I should answer that question. It is the policy of Rights International, Inc., to investigate a complaint, regardless of its origin. Whenever there seems a good reason to do so."

"What was the good reason in this case?"

"The circumstances of the arrest. The world's major airports, Sir Stanley, are in the nature of cosmopolitan places. Dr. Carruthers was arrested there in full international view. I do not find it at all strange that a complaint should have been made."

"In only a few hours?"

"A lot can happen to a man in only a few hours. That is a melancholy fact which we have discovered at Rights International, Inc."

The Commissioner sighed and touched a button on his desk with his knee. He would have been glad if the

meeting he'd just come from had been half as lucid as
the Swede, and he would have been glad if the Swede
had been half as muddled as the Home Secretary.

"What do you want of me then?" he asked.

"Only to speak to Dr. Carruthers. To make sure that
he has not been ill-treated."

"Suppose I were to give you my word?"

"It is another melancholy fact that Rights International,
Inc., has been obliged to draw up strict rules . . ."

"That the prisoner must always be seen?"

"Exactly so, Sir Stanley," replied Palmgren with a self-
deprecatory smile.

The Commissioner knew that he had but a minute or
so to make his decision, before his secretary answered
the call from the knee button. She would give him exactly
five minutes from the moment of the call. The Commissioner had no wish to spend further time with Palmgren,
interesting as the man undoubtedly was. He had to end
the interview decisively one way or the other. At the
moment he opened his mouth to speak, he did not know
in which direction the issue would fall. Then he heard
his own voice.

"I'm afraid it is impossible to grant your request, Mr.
Palmgren. Carruthers died three hours ago."

In the Commissioner's youth, popular writers had often
referred to a person's reactions as being "galvanic." Until
that moment the Commissioner had not properly understood the severity of a true galvanic reaction. Paco Palmgren's whole brain complex suddenly disintegrated, and
in the release of random cerebral impulses his muscles
contracted violently, with the result that he literally leapt
from the chair where he had been sitting, sitting so placidly until this point.

"I would not have believed it . . . here in Britain,"
he stammered, without realising that in so saying much
of his case disintegrated.

"You should read a little of our long and violent history, Mr. Palmgren, and then ask yourself if a leopard really changes its spots."

The Commissioner's secretary, a trim girl with a big bush of natural glossy dark hair, came in.

"Your call is through, Sir," she said. It was a good enough line to enable the Commissioner to bow out the dazed Swede. Sir Stanley used his height in a manner that brooked no further argument.

"Get me General Holland," he snapped when Palmgren had left.

The girl with the black mop skipped hurriedly to the phone, wondering what had got into the Old Man this morning.

London, 17A Courtlane Mews, 10:45 A.M.

Both Hermann Kapp and Anna Morgue had been irritated by the dillydallying of Al Simmonds and Pedro, but they were irritated for different reasons. Both Simmonds and Pedro had insisted on finalising their work on the "thing." To Kapp this seemed quite unnecessary. Simmonds was being fussy, and Pedro, if he really had more work to do, could easily have done it on the previous evening. Kapp certainly had work to do himself because he hadn't finished his trigger design. There were one or two subtleties to it that were still forming in his mind.

Anna Morgue's thoughts were directed very differently. She waited until Simmonds and Pedro had at last gone out by the door which led up from the basement directly into the yard which gave onto the street. Then she let herself into the housekeeper's quarters, to where she would find Sunion Webb. Fate had been a long time catching up with Webb. For a generation he had advocated the overthrow of world governments by violent means. With his sharp nose surmounted by the large horn-rimmed spectacles, with the mane of long white hair brushed straight back from the forehead, with tense body and convinced face, he had argued for violence. Without knowing anything of the true nature of violence. Anna Morgue did not give him very long to learn, because Sunion Webb was not her real quarry. He was merely a means to her real end. Webb saw the tall stringy girl come in through the door of the lounge where he was sitting. He noticed the gun, at first with unconcern. But in a mere fifteen seconds his unconcern passed to incredulity and then to a dark clutching fear. Anna Morgue shot him in the body, and as the head jerked convulsively forward she shot him again in the nape of the neck.

Down in the basement workshop Hermann Kapp heard the shots. Muffled as they were by distance and by the geometry of the house, there was no mistaking the two sharp pulses of sound. In a moment he was up the stairs. The door into the housekeeper's quarters was open. The acrid smell guided him to the lounge. As a boy Hermann Kapp had once watched a pig being slaughtered and had been sickened by the sheer volume of blood which came out of the animal. It was like that now. The freakish thought which ran through his mind was to wonder how the woman managed to keep herself clean, for nowhere on her long housecoat could he see a speck of blood. Feeling half-sick as he had done so many years ago, Kapp started from the lounge, followed closely by Anna Morgue. Suddenly, as if the whole world had lurched off course, Anna Morgue was pointing the gun at *him*. He backed away from it, to find himself in the woman's room. The bed, he noticed, had four corner posts, and knotted to each of them was one end of a long nylon stocking. The other ends of the four stockings lay free upon the bed.

The gun was still on Hermann Kapp. With a twitch

of the barrel the woman ordered him to strip. If it hadn't been for the expression on Anna Morgue's face he would have just laughed, laughed because it was ludicrous. But the eyes didn't permit him to laugh, or even to speak. The light-coloured fleck in one of them seemed more prominent than he had seen it before, and the set look in them suggested drugs. But there had never been any indication that Anna Morgue used drugs. Nor could Hermann Kapp believe she did. Insanity was more likely. Insanity that would undoubtedly make a blood-wrecked corpse out of him, like the little fool of a man in the other room, unless he were to comply with her wishes. So Kapp began to strip off his shirt and trousers.

When he was quite naked, Anna Morgue told him to get himself on the bed and to fasten his own feet to the free ends of two of the nylon stockings. This forced him into a position on his back with his legs apart, which gave him only a poor purchase for resisting her further demands. Resistance became still more difficult when she forced him to fasten one of his own wrists to one of the two remaining stockings. Then she commanded him to lay his free arm on the fourth stocking. As soon as he had complied, she put down the gun, but within easy reach, and quickly knotted the second wrist. There was a brief moment when Hermann Kapp could have hit the woman a sideways blow with his free arm, but it would still have been easy for her to get herself back to the gun. So he hesitated for a moment to think about it, and in that moment she had the remaining wrist loosely fastened. All the stockings were loose, and Kapp realised he was in no danger now if he were to begin to struggle. The woman was enjoying herself tightening the fastenings. She was hard and wiry, but not remotely as strong as the German. Yet he was impeded so seriously by the loose fastenings, which greatly restricted the range of his movements, that it wasn't really possible for him to succeed. And of course if there had been any real possibility of his succeeding, Anna Morgue would simply have returned to the gun. Bit by bit she got the fastenings tighter and tighter, until Hermann Kapp found himself splayed out on his back, as if he were a medieval prisoner staked to the ground.

Very deliberately, she now began to remove the housecoat. She had been wearing nothing at all underneath. She was a stringy bitch all right, not attractive but with enough muscle on her to prevent her from being definitely unattractive. Hermann Kapp's penis had come up while they had been struggling, and it occurred to him that it was lucky it hadn't gone flat down again as soon as she took off the housecoat.

The woman came onto the bed. Instead of starting immediately onto him sexually, she began kneading his muscles, on his arms and legs and on his stomach. The bitch had strong, big hands, and it was as if she was trying to tell him so before she began to work on his penis. He told himself there was nothing to stop him from denying her bringing on his orgasm, and he began to will himself not to let it happen. As if she guessed his thoughts, she began to laugh, and then she began to whisper to him that he would never stop it from coming.

From the time she began to whisper, Hermann Kapp knew he was going. Before he let her bring him quite to the end, he began to whisper back, to whisper that she was a bloody awful skilful bitch. At that she took her hand away and arched her leg over him. He felt his prick go deep inside her. She began to shudder with her thighs, gasping that she would exercise her control over him. Then he was quite gone, and as if his ejection triggered her own orgasm, he felt her thighs stiffen, and even her womb went tight around him for a long moment with everything else gone slack.

Hermann Kapp was surprised to find very little tension left in himself. Then the woman rolled away and unfastened one of his wrists. She left him to untie his legs and the other arm, indeed leaving him alone in the bedroom. As soon as he stood off the bed he noticed the gun, still lying there where she had put it down. He could hear water running in the bathroom, so he thought he would join her there. He couldn't really understand why he should want to join her, unless it was because he didn't want to be alone. But when he went to the bathroom he found the door locked. So he took his clothes to his own bedroom, washed himself down at the hand-basin, dressed, and went back down to the basement workshop. It wasn't until he saw the "thing" assembled there that he remembered the dead man upstairs.

London, Downing Street, 11 A.M.

The Prime Minister had called a mini-Cabinet meeting, ostensibly to discuss procedures for the coming state visit of the French President, but actually to discuss the unwelcome news in the morning paper. He was annoyed, to say the least, by the denial from the Home Secretary because the Prime Minister thought that anybody with even the sense of a medium-sized louse could see that no newspaper would print such details, details like the car and the petrol tank, without having solid proof to back up the story. Henry Fielding was trying his patience more than a bit thin, but the Prime Minister's problem was that, if he gave poor Henry the hoof, who the hell else was to take his place?

None of this irritation showed on the Prime Minister's radiant countenance. The kindly eyes seemed just as kindly as they ever were, and the playful, friendly smile flickered around his mouth, just as it always did.

There was a lot of talk about slapping on D notices.

As well might one seek to shut the stable door after the
horse has left, thought the Prime Minister, and after permitting the discussion of D notices to go on a while longer,
he said so.

Then they all started worrying about blackmail.

"If we give way now," pontificated John Buntingford,
the Foreign Secretary, "we shall never hear the end of
it."

The Prime Minister wondered where poor John had
been all his life. Governments had never been free from
blackmail of one sort and another, ever since the year
dot. Even the strongest and most powerful governments
of the ancient world could be laid low by a series of bad
harvests, by the blackmail of nature. And in modern times
all governments had been blackmailed by weapons tech-
nology, by the demands of rich and poor alike, by the
boll weevil, by everything under the bloody sun. The
Prime Minister thought about saying this too, and then
in pity for poor John, he desisted. Instead, he assumed
his most rubicund expression with the good-king-Wences-
las spirit written all over his beaming face and said, "Well,
then, I think we all agree that at tomorrow's meeting
of the Security Council the British veto will *not* be cast.
And Henry Fielding will of course use all his good offices
to inspire a leak to the press to this effect."

This brought the meeting to a welcome end, leaving
the Prime Minister to congratulate himself on having
managed to avoid referring to the Home Secretary as
"poor Henry."

London, St. John's Wood, Noon

Sir Stanley Farrar stood near the spot in Willy Best's
office where Ernest Carruthers had stood some three
hours earlier in the day. There was a grey, craggy look

in his face which Willy Best had yet to understand. But understanding was not to be long delayed.

"Take him out there. I've had a word with Holland. He'll do the job," the Commissioner said.

There was no smile now on Best's face.

"But Fielding said . . . ," he began.

"It's irrelevant what Fielding said, or what he says. I'm telling you to take him out there. And I've put it in writing for you."

Silently Best took the white envelope which the Commissioner drew from an inside pocket of his coat. Best immediately locked it away in his desk, without opening it. If there were an enquiry, which, of course, there would be, Willy Best wondered if he would bother to open it. Probably he would. Because, unlike the Commissioner, he would be too craven to sacrifice his job.

London, 17A Courtlane Mews, Noon

Al Simmonds and Abu l'Weifa returned to Courtlane Mews with a van, not a saloon car. They had talked together quite a bit in the two-odd hours they'd been together, and they'd decided on the van. Because you could load a heavy thing into a van, whereas a saloon car would have been useless for the idea they both had in mind. They had expected Hermann Kapp to bitch about the van, but to their surprise the German had nodded his approval. Then they had sniffed out the dead man in the housekeeper's lounge, sniffed him out literally. The whiffs of double-based nitro powder and of drying blood were unmistakable to men of their experience. Experience or not, the sight of Sunion Webb took them aback more than a bit.

Al Simmonds wasn't sorry to be rid of the smooth-tongued bastard. In fact, the idea in his head had called

for exactly such a scenario. If it disturbed him, it was
just that the scenario told him more than he liked to
know about the bitch-woman. Simmonds decided that
from here on he would be watching Félix, and not only
out of his eye corners either.

Abu l'Weifa, on the other hand, was concerned by the
death of Sunion Webb, because the little man might conceivably have been useful to the idea which he himself
had in his inner mind. In fact, Abu l'Weifa was not pleased
at all by the little man's death. Webb would have known
quite a lot about how pressure might be put on the British
government. Abu l'Weifa had encountered Left-wing in-
tellectuals before and he knew they had their uses. And
now this little man who lay there on the carpet, drenched
in a cascade of his own blood, would be of no use to
anybody anymore. In his mind the scene called forth a
certain passage in the Koran which he thought he had
long forgotten. He gave his deep, throaty chuckle as he
went out from the housekeeper's lounge, but there was
nothing of humour in the chuckle.

The three men who now went to work had very different ideas on how they intended to make use of the
"thing," but on one subject at least they were entirely
in agreement—on the need to get the "thing" and themselves away from 17A Courtlane Mews just as soon as
they possibly could. So long as they were working for
Sunion Webb and for the people who stood behind him
the house could be considered "safe." But the house
would be safe now only for as long as the people behind
Webb remained in ignorance of his death. The three men
had more than a suspicion that the people behind Sunion
Webb disposed of a very long arm indeed, and they had
no intention of waiting around there for that arm to take
them all by the throat.

But getting Little Boy, as Simmonds kept remembering

the people at Los Alamos had called just such a "thing," up the flight of stone steps from the basement workshop into the yard above, and of then lifting him into the van, called for some thinking. Little Boy weighed more than a ton, and being bright and shiny, he would be very visible to the world outside.

So the first step was to swaddle Little Boy in plenty of packing. The workshop being deficient in soft materials, they fetched blankets from the bedrooms. After wrappings of blankets they finished off Little Boy by winding a small carpet around his cylindrical body, fastening it tightly with lengths of steel wire.

The reason why Al Simmonds and Abu l'Weifa had taken so long to return with the van was that they had already addressed themselves to the problem of the flight of stone steps. After hiring the van itself, they had spent a further hour driving around until they had happened on a suitable small pulley block and rope attachment, which they had "borrowed" from a building site, the third site they had visited.

The pulley block did not solve the problem entirely, however, because the pulley block had to be hooked to a secure fixture. The back axle of the van would have done for that, but Hermann Kapp turned the scheme down flat. It would mean standing in the yard with the pulley block exposed for every passerby in the street outside to see. With two men hauling hard on it, merely to lift an apparent roll of carpet, the operation would look so obviously ridiculous that it would be certain to attract attention. So Kapp said, and the others were reluctantly forced to agree with him.

There was nothing to be done but to make a fixture inside the van itself, so that the pulley block and the men hauling on it would be inside the van, out of sight of casual passersby. So Simmonds took an electric drill

with a long power cable up to the van to drill holes in
the van floor, so as to be able to bolt down a plate there,
a plate with an eye attachment on it.

Hermann Kapp wasn't worried about this part of the
job because people were given to working on vehicles
in the Mews all the time. It was the length of time Simmonds took over the job which worried him. But Simmonds wanted to make sure the floor of the van would
be strong enough, and he wasn't happy about it. Was
Simmonds ever happy about any job? Hermann Kapp
fretted. Then the plate with the eye attachment had
to be made up and that too seemed to take an age. It
was already coming up to three o'clock by the time Simmonds grudgingly admitted to being finished with the
job.

They backed the van as close as they could to the top
of the stone steps, and Hermann Kapp had them bring
out a dozen or so articles of furniture from the house
which they dumped close by the open back of the van.
He told Félix to keep on bringing out a few more articles,
and then went with Pedro into the van, leaving Simmonds to guide Little Boy up the stone steps. The angle
of the steps was quite steep, so the two men had to pull
hard on the rope through the pulley block, and all the
while Simmonds kept shouting instructions to them as
he eased Little Boy from one position to another. Luckily,
Félix had the wit to keep shouting back to Simmonds
in raucous French, which performance would be more
likely to hold the attention of any curious person than
the roll of carpet itself. The last bit of the job was a vertical
lift of about three feet, up into the van itself, and of course
then to secure Little Boy so that he wouldn't roll about
all over the floor of the van. Al Simmonds used a number
of wedges to deal with this last detail. Meanwhile, the
other three busied themselves in carrying the articles
of furniture back again into the house—so far as casual

passersby in the street were concerned, it now looked as if they were unloading the furniture from the van.

With the moment of leaving 17A Courtlane Mews close at hand, Hermann Kapp forced himself to check and to double-check. To check he had the papers which Webb had given him, that he had all his own personal papers, including his maps of London, that he had left nothing back there in the house which might serve later to identify him to the police. He was anxious to be away, but these last precautions were time well spent. The others saw him making these checks and they too started to clear up their personal effects. Al Simmonds even thought about fingerprints, but decided that his own must be distributed so liberally around the workshop that it would be impossible to remove them all. Not for the first time he regretted his inability to wear gloves, but wearing gloves always destroyed the sensitivity of his fingers, causing him to become unbearably irritated. So Simmonds simply contented himself with retrieving his own bag and with filling a second bag with food from the kitchen. Not that the sight of the dead man had made him ravenous with hunger, but hunger would assuredly come later, he decided.

Simmonds and Abu l'Weifa climbed into the back of the van to keep an eye on Little Boy. It had been Hermann Kapp's intention to drive, but when he came out of the house he found Félix in the driver's seat. He thought about asking if she had a suitable license, and then decided not to bother. He noticed it was just after 4 P.M. as they pulled away from 17A Courtlane Mews.

Hemel Hempstead Area, 4 P.M.

Willy Best paced about the concrete floor of what seemed to be a storeroom, just as he had done for the past two hours. Following his midday meeting with the

Commissioner, he had put a call through to Barry Gwent. There had been nothing else for him to do, for although the Commissioner had told him to take Carruthers "out there," he had no idea where "out there" might be. It hadn't escaped Best that both Barry Gwent and General Holland had troubled themselves to come to St. John's Wood. To prevent him from discovering the whereabouts of their HQ, he had decided.

So he'd tried to call Gwent, but had been put through to General Holland instead. The General had told him to bring Carruthers in a police vehicle to a transfer point, at an ordnance map position to the south of King's Langley. Then Carruthers had put up his usual ineffectual physical demonstration, and it had been necessary to handcuff him. They had manhandled the fellow into a cage in the back of a police van. Willy Best had gone along in the front seat of the van with the absurd thought running in his head that now he understood better than he'd ever done before why experienced criminals always "went quietly." Being docile gave them the best chance of escape in the event of an unexpected accident, an act of God, as you might say. Act of God or not, Willy Best could see no escape now for Carruthers.

At the transfer point Carruthers had been hustled into a military car. The MI people obviously would have been glad to "lose" the police entirely at that stage, but it had been essentially impossible for them not to bring along Best himself. They had put him in the back of the big car along with the handcuffed Carruthers, and with two hard-faced types sitting immediately opposite on let-down seats. Partly because the hard-faced types always seemed to be in his range of vision, and partly because the side windows had blinds drawn, Best could only judge vaguely the route from the ordnance marking to the HQ. He knew they were somewhere west of Hemel

Hempstead, not too far from Great Missingden, he would have guessed.

The HQ turned out to be an old-style country manor house with several huts of a temporary character nearby. Carruthers had been taken immediately away, and Best had been brought to one of the huts, to the storeroom where he had spent the past two hours. He tried to fill his mind with inconsequential things, like the tracing of this HQ. He reckoned it would be about a half afternoon's job for the police. Just a few calls around the country villages would do the trick. Sooner or later a country bobby would come on the phone, knowing all about it, a bobby who to this point had been in the habit of turning his head the other way. There were some things the police could do well, and some things the military could do that the police couldn't. Which was why it was necessary to have both. Both the police and this branch of MI were under the Home Office, but without any direct connexion between them. The connexions were vertical, up from the Commissioner and General Holland directly to the Home Secretary, not horizontally between Willy Best and Barry Gwent. Best thought about that, and it didn't take him long to decide he was glad it was that way.

By now, four o'clock, his mouth was as dry as hot sand. He wasn't easy in any of his thoughts. In fact, he hated the position he'd got himself into, to a point where after all his years in the force he wondered if he was in the right job after all. Maybe he should have allowed Carruthers a lawyer? The question tormented him. A sensible lawyer might have persuaded the man to come out with the information the easy way. But it would have been necessary to use an independent lawyer, not a lawyer of Carruthers' choice. A lawyer of Carruthers' choice would only too likely have ruined any chance there was

of getting the information. And an independent lawyer
would hardly have done any better than he could do
himself. At least he persuaded himself that this was so.

Willy Best wondered what else he could have done
in the circumstances. His brain was seeking to pull this
problem to pieces when Barry Gwent and another man
came into the hut. Gwent had a sheet of paper in his
hand.

"I think this is what you were after," he said, handing
the paper to Best.

"He didn't last as far as the second injection," grinned
the other man. With a shock, Best realised the fellow
was really only a young lad.

"At least he didn't have anything else to offer on the
second," Gwent continued. Willy Best thought he was
going to be sick. Hard buggers, he thought to himself,
bloody hard buggers. Then he looked more carefully at
the paper. Seven London addresses had been neatly
typed on it. Bloody neat typing, Best's mind continued
to stutter internally to himself.

"Are we going to take him back to St. John's Wood?"
he managed to ask.

"He's going to be held here for the time being," Barry
Gwent replied. "General Holland arranged it with the
Commissioner," he went on, noticing the expression on
the policeman's face.

Willy Best suddenly wanted to be away from the place,
away now with his sheet of paper. Then his long training
reasserted itself.

"Have you a phone?" he asked.

The two men took him to a much smaller room in
the same temporary building where a solitary phone
stood on a small table.

"The switchboard will handle the calls if you give them
the numbers," Barry Gwent told him. Then the two men

went out, and as they walked back to the manor house, Gwent said to his young companion, "Soft. Amazing, isn't it? He'd have half London blown sky-high before he'd put this Carruthers even into a dentist's chair."

London, The Home Office, 4 P.M.

Sir Stanley Farrar followed behind Henry Fielding's PPS. He had been summoned to the Home Office, to appear there at four o'clock sharp. He was in little doubt about what the topic would be. The only question was whether or not he would find Paco Palmgren together with the Home Secretary. His estimation of the Home Secretary's character was that Fielding would conduct the interview in front of Palmgren, to assure the Swede that he himself had been no party to the Carruthers affair.

And of course Paco Palmgren was indeed there, in discussion with the Home Secretary.

"I want an immediate verbal report on the condition of Dr. Ernest Carruthers," the Home Secretary began, "and I want a full written report at the earliest possible moment."

The Commissioner stood, holding his cap on one arm as he had often done in earlier years.

"What in particular do you want to know about Dr. Carruthers?"

"Where he is, for God's sake, and his condition."

"To the best of my knowledge, Sir, he is at present being interrogated by one of General Holland's units. What his condition may be, I cannot say."

The Home Secretary half-sprung from his chair. Then he collapsed back down, his face suddenly very pale.

"I gave no such order," he said in a throaty, strangled voice.

"General Holland is a responsible officer, Sir," the Commissioner replied, determined not to let the Home Secretary off the hook of his own making, for the Commissioner was angry to be drawn up like that, like an errant schoolboy, in front of this Swede.

Henry Fielding grabbed a phone from his desk, and snapped, "Get me General Holland."

"Who is General Holland?" Palmgren asked.

"I would advise you to avoid falling into his hands, Mr. Palmgren," the Commissioner smiled as grimly as he felt.

"Mr. Fielding, you gave me assurances . . . ," Palmgren began.

"This is no part of my doing!" the Home Secretary shouted, his face changing quickly from white to red. Like the wine at one of his dinner parties, the Commissioner thought to himself.

"But after your assurances what need is there for this General Holland?" The Swede did not let much get past him. Clever man. Which was exactly why he was there, of course. The Commissioner's mind flickered over the conditions of the Official Secrets Act. Odd how it could be construed against almost everything you said. But to hell with that. Like Macbeth, he was already too deep in blood to turn back.

"General Holland is a member of the Home Secretary's staff," he said to Palmgren.

"Is this so, Mr. Fielding?"

Henry Fielding could not deny it was so, but neither would he make such a damaging admission to the Swede. So he simply sat there, his mouth half-open like a stranded fish, the Commissioner thought.

Palmgren made a sudden decision. He drew himself to formal attention, remembering in time not to click his heels, and said in a toneless voice, as if he were making challenge to a duel, "Then I will be leaving, Mr. Fielding.

I think neither you nor your government will like my report very much."

Palmgren swung round to go, but the Commissioner called him back.

"Mr. Palmgren, I'd advise you to be out of the country before midnight," he said in a quiet voice.

Palmgren squared up his strong shoulders, and then came up close to the Commissioner.

"And why should that be? What sort of a country is this?" he asked.

"A soft country, but not yet so soft that we can't move to protect ourselves when the occasion demands it," was the reply.

"And what now demands it?"

"You should put that question to your masters in Moscow, Mr. Palmgren."

Palmgren nodded, almost bowed.

"My masters in Moscow! Is that it? *I* have no masters in Moscow."

"Then I'd advise you to make a trip *there*, Mr. Palmgren. On behalf of Rights International, Inc."

Palmgren walked for the second time toward the door. Pausing for an instant before he went out, he said, "We do not like what goes on in Moscow either."

"Are you mad?" the Home Secretary shouted as soon as the Swede had closed the door. Then the phone rang and as Fielding picked it up the Commissioner could hear the characteristic resonances of General Holland's voice coming faintly to him from the earpiece.

Even though the conversation which followed was evidently torrid, the Commissioner only half-listened to it. Holland was plainly taking a strong line, and that was sufficient for the Commissioner. He had come there with the full intention of turning in his resignation. Indeed, he had it all written out in a white envelope in an inner pocket of his uniform, the full uniform which he had put on specially for the occasion. But as events had progressed, the Commissioner had decided he was damned if he was going to make it easy for Fielding. He would force the Home Secretary to dismiss him. And now, with Holland pitching a strong line, he doubted that Fielding would have the guts to suspend him.

London, Courtlane Mews, 5 P.M.

Two young police constables turned into Courtlane Mews. All they knew was that a message from their local station had told them to go immediately to 17A, and to take a look there, but with some caution. They did not know that Chief Superintendent Willy Best had telephoned similar messages to six other police districts in the metropolitan area. If they had known this, then doubtless they would have asked themselves just why the Super was in such a rush, and doubtless they would have been a good deal more circumspect in their approach to 17A. Both of them knew the Mews. So far as they were aware, there was nothing particularly suspicious about the place, not more so than anywhere else in their district.

They took a general look at 17A from the outside. Nobody inside, so far as they could tell. One of them rang the doorbell while the other stood a little way off across the street watching the house windows. When there was no reply, the constable at the door rang the bell again. Still no reply. So now a very long ring. Still no reply. Evidently, nobody at home. The door was locked, as they expected it to be. The two constables conferred together for a moment. Then one of them, the one who had been standing in the street and who had noticed the stone steps in the yard, began to go down toward the basement.

"Something has been brought up here," he shouted to his companion as he removed pieces of a fluffy material from several of the sharp stone edges. "Looks like bits of carpet," said his companion, after examining the fluff. Then they tried the basement door. They found it unlocked, for Hermann Kapp had forgotten to bother himself with it. Once they had the light on in the basement, the two constables knew they had found something much more than a bit suspicious—something suspicious was what the sergeant at the station had said to look for.

The two constables browsed about the basement for a few moments, savouring the taste of discovery. Then they stamped upstairs. There was a smell about the place they didn't like, and in what seemed only a few seconds they found themselves staring down at the grotesquely sprawled body of Sunion Webb.

London, The Embankment, 6 P.M.

Anna Morgue had found a place to park for the time that Hermann Kapp wanted. Why he wanted to stop there on the busy Embankment and why he was intently examining the opposite side of the river she simply could not understand.

Hermann Kapp's sight was good, but even so he felt the lack of binoculars. It was ridiculous not to have binoculars, such a simple thing at such a critical moment. He strolled up and down the sidewalk, close to the wall which separated the sidewalk from the river. A number of old-style sailing ships were moored nearby. Why they were there baffled and worried him. He took a good look at the ships, and decided at last that they would probably not interfere with his plan. Several people strolled by carrying binoculars. Hermann Kapp thought about asking to borrow one of them for a minute or two, and then he decided reluctantly not to draw attention to himself by doing so.

He guessed that Al Simmonds and Pedro were surely becoming uneasy about Little Boy, for how could it be otherwise for them, being bedded down with such a thing in the back of the van? This too fitted well with his plan. As for Félix, he was not sure what she thought about Little Boy. But this was irrelevant, because Félix played no role where decisions on the disposition of Little Boy were concerned. Yet it was through Little Boy that the something between them would finally be resolved. So Hermann Kapp had decided.

London, 17A Courtlane Mews, 6 P.M.

In spite of an excellent driver, in spite of the sophistication of the electronic equipment with which his car was equipped, in spite of receiving by radio at an early stage the news of the discovery made by the two young constables, it took Willy Best nearly an hour and a half to make the forty-odd miles from the region of Hemel Hempstead to 17A Courtlane Mews. Such was the traffic paralysis of the greater city of London, a paralysis which successive civil administrations had not sought to relieve, except by measures that were obviously ineffective from the moment of their conception.

By the time Best arrived at 17A Courtlane Mews, police photographers were at work in the housekeeper's lounge, for it was the corpse of Sunion Webb which seemed to have a fascination for them all. Cluny Robertson was busying himself in directing the angles of the photographs.

Sir Stanley Farrar, the Commissioner, arrived at six o'clock. The Commissioner at least had the elementary sense to realise that the basement workshop was the place of greatest importance and interest. Could a bomb have been assembled there? Undoubtedly yes, Willy Best told himself. Had a bomb been assembled there? From the tailings scattered around the machines, the steel chips shining and new, the answer to this second question seemed also to be yes. How long ago had the bomb been assembled? This was more difficult, and Willy Best conferred with the Commissioner about it. Then one of the two young constables who had found the basement workshop came up and told him about the bits of fluff on the stone steps outside. So Willy Best and the Commissioner examined the stone steps, and as they did so it gradually became clear that while they were too late, they were not many hours too late. The Commissioner cursed himself to himself. Had he made his decision about Carruthers half a day sooner, they would not have been too late.

Meanwhile the Super told every spare man he could find to go up and down the Mews to discover what the people living there could remember. Had a vehicle recently carried away a large heavy object? And if so, could anyone be found who remembered its registration number? Within half an hour Best had answers that were said to relate to a furniture removal van which had parked by the house for several hours. But unfortunately the answers were by no means precise. Yet there were similarities, and by putting the similarities together, Willy Best arrived at what he hoped was a tolerable approximation to the truth, particularly the truth about the registration number of the vehicle. Then he had the number radioed to stations everywhere throughout greater London.

London, The Thames River, 7 P.M.

Once the heavy afternoon commuter rush had eased away, the London traffic fell to an unusually low volume. Although repeated broadcasts on radio and television had

stressed that absolutely no officially known threat to the
city existed, people who were in a position to do so had
nevertheless been leaving steadily throughout the day.
Better to be safe than sorry was their motto. And as Hermann Kapp had instantly guessed, there had been widespread cancellations of foreign airline flights into London.
These several factors had all contributed to the evening
traffic being at a low ebb.

In Fleet Street, Jack Hart, Stan Tambling, and the Chief
Editor of their paper were not quite in the exultant mood
of the previous evening, because during the day there
had been widespread threats of heavy civil actions against
the paper. The paper's lawyers had spent the whole day
considering the complex ramifications of the affair.

The government had not slapped on D notices, because
to have done so would in effect have confirmed the verac-
ity of the original story. So with the damage done, all
the other papers in the city were now in high spirits as
they sought in less dramatic ways to add fuel to the flames.

Although the evening traffic volume was low, there
were still many young people driving exultantly about
the streets, for the possibility that a nuclear bomb might
have been assembled in their midst added a strange and
urgent spice to the process of living. What they had to
do they had better do quickly, many of them decided.
So it was not in a London by any means deserted of all
traffic that Anna Morgue drove Little Boy and her three
companions across Waterloo Bridge to the south side of
the Thames river. Under Hermann Kapp's guidance she
turned immediately left into Stamford Street. Then she
made a short jog, again to the left, into a smaller street
which ran parallel to the river. Along this smaller street
Kapp told her to go very slowly in a direction away from
Waterloo Bridge.

Between the street and the river was a tangle of ware-

houses, jetties, and slipways. Hermann Kapp called on
Félix to stop while he examined an old sign which read
Barge House Street. Then he had a hurried conversation
with the two men in the back, assuring them that everything was O.K. A few yards further on he found the place
he had picked out on the map, a narrow street set between warehouses, a street that went right to the river
edge itself. Halfway along the street, however, was a tall,
locked iron gate. Anna Morgue brought the van to a stop
just short of the iron gate, and then Kapp told them all
that before they could make their next move they must
wait a couple of hours, until the light of day began to
fade. Meanwhile Al Simmonds might amuse himself in
forcing the lock on the iron gate, quietly, though.

Simmonds thought that for the moment he'd got something much better to do, for by now the hunger he'd
long anticipated was on him. He produced the bag of
food, offering it round to the others also. Abu l'Weifa
and Anna Morgue ate moderately, but Hermann Kapp
would eat nothing at all. This left most of it for Simmonds
himself, and he was glad of that. Politeness hadn't cost
him too much, he decided.

With his hunger satisfied, and with the tools which his
foresight had told him to bring along, the iron gate was
an easy matter. In fact, it was only a bolt and padlock,
with the padlock so large that you could almost get your
fingers into it. Simmonds had it open in five minutes,
feeling almost insulted that his skill should be called on
to effect such a trivial job. Even the bloody bitch-woman
could have done it, even without using her gun. Then
Simmonds returned to the van to wait out the time until
they were ready for the next move.

By now Abu l'Weifa had found plenty of time to think
his innermost thoughts. He'd no real grounds for being
suspicious of Hermann Kapp, but his own motives and

those of Kapp were different. Abu l'Weifa felt himself
to be an important part of a newly emerging culture.
Kapp had no such ambitions. Kapp was a clever operator
but a floater with no depth to him. He was clever, the
next move in this game of his was clever. Abu l'Weifa
could see it coming now, and he approved of it. But there
was one critical thing about Little Boy of which he didn't
approve. And, again, this wasn't personal against Hermann Kapp. It was technical, in a way that neither Al
Simmonds nor the woman could understand, not unless
the basic principles were carefully explained to them.

Abu l'Weifa understood chemical explosives very
clearly. An explosive was an unstable substance which
changed to a more stable substance in the very moment
of its explosion, and it was this change which supplied
the outbursts of energy which had made the bombs of
Abu l'Weifa into social weapons of great power. Making
an unstable substance like this wasn't a matter of any
great difficulty, because there were lots of them. But most
were too unstable, too fickle, too ready to go off when
you were not ready for them to go off. So the great discovery in the history of explosives had been to produce a
few substances that would not go off until they received
a violent shock. When once they were going they went;
there was no stopping them. The kind of plastic explosive
that Abu l'Weifa liked to use could be kneaded in your
hand to any shape you liked. You could drop it on the
floor, jump on it, or throw it against a wall, and the shock
of that wasn't sufficient to set it off. By itself, it was safe
stuff to have around.

But once your main explosive was supplied with a detonator you had to be much more careful. A detonator
was just another unstable chemical, but a much less con-
trollable one than the main explosive. Quite often it was
fulminate of mercury, which had been used for many

centuries. Any sudden impulse, like treading on it, or throwing it against a wall, or heating it with an electric current, would set off the detonator, and once the detonator was gone the main explosive was gone.

An electric current flowing from an internal battery, or along wires from outside, was the usual way to set off a bomb. With an internal battery, the moment of explosion, the moment when the electric current was made to flow by closing a switch, could be decided by a clock, which you put in the bomb. Or it could be decided by arranging some mechanical trip device, the way you did with a booby trap. Or it could be done in the most crude way of all, by a corrosive chemical eating its way through a diaphragm. But internal mechanisms had a big disadvantage for Abu l'Weifa, because once they were set they were set. For just the opposite reason internal mechanisms were attractive to beginners, because after setting his bomb, a beginner could run away and make himself safe before the bomb explosion occurred. But how could an internally set bomb be used to select a particular car out of a whole motorcade, the particular car with the ministers in it, leaving it a twisted mass of metal at the bottom of a twenty-yard crater? Never could it be done that way. You had to have external wires. Then, at exactly the right moment, you yourself could close the circuit. So it was all under control. Eh?

Little Boy was similar to an ordinary bomb in quite a few respects. Little Boy had the usual detonator to be activated by an electric current, and it had a main chemical to be exploded by the detonator. But it also had a third explosive of a quite different kind, not a chemical explosive at all. This was the uranium, which would become enormously explosive once the two pieces of it were brought together into a neat sphere. The main chemical explosion served to do this, to bring the pieces of uranium together. But the chemical explosive did not itself start up the nuclear explosion of the uranium, not at all in the manner of a detonator. It was the neutron source which Hermann Kapp had been so careful about that would start up the nuclear explosion. Yet although Little Boy had this fantastic nuclear addition to the ordinary bomb, it was still dependent in the usual way on an ordinary chemical detonator—a detonator like fulminate of mercury. It was the ordinary chemical detonator which would set going the whole chain of operations. And the chemical detonator needed an electric current, but not an electric current in the usual way, and it was precisely on this particular abnormality that Abu l'Weifa's thoughts were centred.

Little Boy could not be set internally, because then it would explode willy-nilly, and that would make it entirely useless as a blackmail device. Nor could an electric current be sent to it along wires from outside, as Abu l'Weifa had done so recently in Madrid. The reason you couldn't do this was that the wires would be impossibly long, assuming you yourself retreated away from the bomb to a safe distance. A radio signal to Little Boy was the answer to this further problem, and this involved the further step of adding a radio amplifier, a radio amplifier powered by an internal battery. But the solution of this further problem raised yet another problem. You were not the only person to be sending radio signals. Radio signals of all kinds were being broadcast all the time, by broadcasting corporations, the military, the police, taxis, aircraft—there was almost no end to it. To stop an unwanted explosion from occurring due to all these indiscriminate radio signals, it had been necessary to fit Little Boy with a coded gate or key. Only a radio signal preceded by the right code could activate the bomb.

Abu l'Weifa had no objection to the place where Hermann Kapp would surely be putting the bomb. Any suitably concealed place in London was O.K. by him. His problem was, first, to acquire the code, and then, second, to rid himself of his present company. For Abu l'Weifa could see plainly that his present company had no burning interest in Spain, or in Morocco, or in any of the other two or three issues which he himself thought important. Hence it followed that before he himself could make use of Little Boy the team must be changed. There had to be quite different faces on the job. The previous evening when he had largely finished his work on Little Boy, when he had lounged in apparent nonchalance about the basement workshop, Abu l'Weifa had in fact been keeping an acute watch on the German. He had seen enough to understand the general nature of the radio device which Hermann Kapp had built for Little Boy. This was just the point. He understood only the general nature, not the precise nature, as he would have to do eventually. He would need to know the precise code, and he would need to make sure that the use of Little Boy fell exclusively to him, not to the others. What was it they wanted of Little Boy? Money? For Al Simmonds, yes. Terror for terror's sake, for the woman, perhaps. For Hermann Kapp? Abu l'Weifa had no real answer to Kapp, and this was his second problem. The code first, and Kapp second.

Moscow, 10 P.M.

There were five of them in the Chairman's apartments, the Chairman himself, two Politburo colleagues, Valas Georgian, and Igor Markov. Throughout the day the British political scene had been closely monitored. Following the British Cabinet meeting in the morning, there had been increasingly clear hints that the British veto would not be cast on the following day. The suggestions that it would not be cast had already come in the afternoon from "political observers in Whitehall." The afternoon radio bulletins had all mentioned it, and by evening it had become a main news item on the British television transmissions. So the five men in the Chairman's apartments knew that, as near as a high probability can be to a certainty, their plans had succeeded. Or, more accurately, the plan of Igor Markov had succeeded.

The number of toasts which had been drunk were taking the edge off Markov's perceptions, and he was a little glad that this was so, for not quite everything he had learned over the past few hours was comfortable in its implications. There should have been an early afternoon report from the Englishman, Sunion Webb. When none had come through, Markov had taken the sensible step of putting an observer onto 17A Courtlane Mews. He had received two messages from the observer, one telling him of the van and the movements of furniture in and out of the house. The other report had been of the arrival of the English police. It had been a mighty relief to Igor Markov to hear of the dead man who had then been taken away. The dead man for a certainty would be Sunion Webb. Webb had in any case been an important loose end to the operation, important because Webb was a connexion to Moscow, and an "end" because ends had always to be tied up.

The first of the two messages had made it clear to Igor Markov that the bomb itself had been removed from 17A Courtlane Mews. So what, he had asked himself. The people who now had possession of it were in no way connected with his own organisation. They had been hired for the job. Not a single component of the bomb was of Soviet manufacture. True, the uranium was of

Soviet production, but uranium in one country was the same as uranium in another country. Except that perhaps the enrichment factors were different. But Igor Markov had seen that one, clearly and distinctly, even from the beginning. Once he had seen the point, it had been easy for the chemists to make up specimens with an enrichment factor agreeing with an American production value. Everything was easy, so long as you saw the point soon enough.

The most awkward loose end had indeed been the bomb itself. Markov's plan for coping with that had been in slow tempo. Just to have the caretakers of 17A Courtlane Mews return there. To have them live quietly, perhaps for as long as a year, and then for two or three of his own technicians to move in and dismantle the thing. But now he was saved even that trouble. The way it had turned out, no linkages had been left, except for the circumstances of the acquisition of the house by the Anglo-Soviet Peace Association. But even that acquisition had been done by an Englishman, so the linkage there was weak. Cynically it could be said to be more Anglo than Soviet. The association itself would suffer, of course, which was a pity, because such associations sometimes had remarkable uses. But surely the loss there did not outweigh the gain.

Igor Markov jerked himself away from these thoughts, for it had come round again to his turn to propose a toast. He raised his glass of clear cold vodka high in front of his face, and with a smile he proposed, "To the next time."

London, Scotland Yard, 8 P.M.

Willy Best and the Commissioner stood in front of the big wall map in the communications room. Best thought

that now, if ever at any time in his life, was the moment
for a grand inspiration, the sort of inspiration which the
great detectives of fiction were always having. But how
the hell did you locate an unknown number of people,
of unknown names and unknown appearances, somewhere in the whole of London? The answer was that
you didn't, except by a freak chance. And the only freak
chance that Willy Best could see was the van which had
carried a ghastly, unspeakable thing away from the basement of 17A Courtlane Mews. The freak possibility that
he had guessed the registration number of the van correctly. He had every available patrol car out looking for
a van with that guessed number.

London, The Thames River, 8:15 P.M.

Hermann Kapp had carefully walked the short distance
from the van to the edge of the river. He had paused
for a moment to move the iron gate backward and forward a little. The squeak from its hinges was audible
but not overwhelmingly so. The gate was evidently in
use, and this was important for the next move, because
the slipway into the river, the slipway which he had noted
from the northern side of the river, would then also be
in use. He had feared it might be in a decayed condition,
and since he was anxious to avoid bumping Little Boy
too much, because of the unstable fulminate in the first
of its three linked explosive stages, a broken-up kind of
slipway would have been bad.

He wondered why the thought of an inadvertent explosion of Little Boy worried him more than a small ordinary
bomb would have done. The result for him could only
be the same. He couldn't suffer more than death. Being
cooked to millions of degrees was no worse than being

cooked to a thousand degrees. It was all very ridiculous, he decided.

He was also worried by the thought that they might be seen by people looking across at them from the other side of the river. His first plan had been to wait until after daylight had gone. There would still be sufficient artificial light from the city itself for them to do the job. But then he'd remembered how visibility always seems to be at its worst just before the last of the daylight. After dark the eyes actually become more acute and more perceptive again. When he'd finished examining the riverside, Hermann Kapp reckoned they had about half an hour to effect the dumping of Little Boy. He also reckoned that since the slipway was smooth and at a good angle, about twenty degrees, there would be less than a 1000-lb. strain on the rope which would hold Little Boy on his descent into the river.

Kapp walked back to the van and took the driver's position now. Al Simmonds opened the iron gate, taking care to do it bit by bit, so that the gate didn't squeak too much. And the van had to be turned and backed up so that the rear end of it opened directly onto the slipway. Because Kapp knew exactly what manoeuvre he wanted, there was no difficulty in it.

Since everybody was anxious to be rid of Little Boy, there was no argument from anyone about the dumping. Hermann Kapp left Al Simmonds and Pedro to get on with it, with lowering Little Boy onto the slipway, with letting him then roll gently down into the river, and down further into deeper water. He would be nicely camouflaged there in his protective roll of carpet. Anna Morgue went back to the iron gate to make sure they were not inconvenienced, while Hermann Kapp opened up his case. There was one last detail for him to attend to. It

was a detail that scared him to the depths of his being,
but do it he must because it was to be his final reckoning
with Félix.

Kapp's nerves were suddenly shattered by a high-
pitched wail of agony from the interior of the van. With
shaking hands he returned the instruments to his case.
He had to be exceedingly careful about the instruments.
This was made infinitely hard for him by the noise which
didn't go away. With the instruments safely stored it took
but a second or two for Kapp to run round to the rear
of the van. He was in time to see Little Boy running
freely on the slipway. The thing entered the water just
as he caught sight of it, and the water then quickly slowed
its speed. Even so, Kapp felt certain it would be moving
too fast when it reached the river bottom. The fulminate
would go with the shock of it, and with the fulminate
everything would go. But by the time these thoughts
had run through his fuddled mind, Little Boy was down
there in the water, and nothing had happened. Except
that from inside the van the wailing continued.

As Hermann Kapp reached the back of the van, Abu
l'Weifa climbed out. A glance inside showed him that
the plate bolted to the van floor had moved, the hook
of the pulley block had come clear of the eye in the
plate, and with a 1000-lb. tension on it the hook had
essentially severed the left arm of Al Simmonds.

Whatever the weakness that Anna Morgue had discovered in him, during the next hour Hermann Kapp showed
exactly why he was the leader. He wound a length of
rope around Simmonds' upper arm, just below the shoulder. He twisted it and tightened it as much as he could,
and then he told Abu l'Weifa to make sure it didn't loosen.
Next he threw the pulley block and its attachments into
the river. Lastly he fastened up the rear of the van. He
told Anna Morgue to close the gate, and to make sure

it was properly locked. He drove the van himself through
the gate and up the street to where a lamp gave sufficient
light to read the map. By the time Anna Morgue came
up with him, he had found the position of a nearby hospital in Stamford Street. Anna Morgue remembered driving
past it, so he let her drive again. Simmonds was still wailing in a nightmare world of his own. So Kapp leaned
over into the back of the van and told Abu l'Weifa that
they would soon be at the hospital. A moment later they
came into Stamford Street and began to search for the
hospital. Then just as Hermann Kapp felt he would get
there in time there came a harsh groan and a kind of
bubbling sound from Simmonds. Seconds later, Abu
l'Weifa's face appeared and whispered to him that Simmonds was dead.

If it hadn't been for Little Boy, Kapp would have told
Anna Morgue to stop. But just now he wanted to be out
of London as quickly as possible. So he let her drive on
into Waterloo Road again, where they turned left toward
south London. Half a mile along they came to a kind
of plaza with several streets opening off it. They took
what seemed to be the street which kept to the original
direction. Hermann Kapp looked about him to discover
the name of the street, and it was then that he noticed
the winking roof light of a police car. At the same moment
he heard the siren start up.

Hermann Kapp had long since learned that the one
thing to avoid, when a police car starts a pursuit not
far behind you, is the hope that the fellow is after someone
else. You know for sure that he's after you, and you take
action accordingly. The action to be taken depends on
your vehicle. If it is fast enough, you try to outrun the
man behind. If it isn't fast enough, you stop instantly—
there is no point at all in continuing until the fellow comes
up behind you. Then he's got you, and the situation is

not good, especially if your clothes are blood spattered
and you have a dead man lolling in the back of your
vehicle.

"Police!" he shouted. "I'm taking the wheel."

Kapp steered the van toward the middle of the road.
Judging the manoeuvre to be just possible, he screamed
"Brake hard!" in Anna Morgue's ear, and continued to
pull the van directly in front of the incoming traffic. All
over the street there was a loud screaming of brakes.
The van came to a shuddering stop, and Kapp was out
of it still with his case, shouting, "Out! Out!" to his aston-
ished companions. Anna Morgue caught up with him as
he reached the sidewalk. Then he saw Pedro come running, and what he saw he didn't like. For Pedro had a
dark stain across his front, both pants and shirt. The only
good thing about it was that in the street lights the stain
looked brown, not bright red.

It is very natural to have one's attention riveted by
the unusual rather than by the usual, and a van slewing
across the street in front of oncoming cars is far more
unusual than three people trotting on the sidewalk, especially if the van turns out to have a dead man inside it.
Hermann Kapp knew this full well, but he also knew
that people in nearby cars now stopped in the street must
have seen the three of them jump from the van. So after
quickly making about fifty yards, he led the other two
to the other side of the street, threading his way in a
complex pattern through the now stationary traffic. There
were many openings into smaller, darker streets and passageways, and it was into one of these that he soon turned.
Less than two minutes had elapsed since Hermann Kapp
had noticed the police car.

Much had been lost. The police had been an hour behind them at 17A Courtlane Mews. Now their advantage
had been whittled down to a mere few seconds. Hermann

Kapp's quick thinking had seemingly widened that slender margin a bit, but their position was not good, not good at all, not with Pedro looking like a butcher's apprentice, and with Hermann Kapp himself in no pristine condition. Their only assets were the case which he himself had grabbed in the last moment and the handbag which Anna Morgue never let out of her possession. Pedro-the-fool had left his bag behind in the van. Hermann Kapp found himself wondering what documents Pedro might have in his bag. He decided he would like to dump Pedro the way they'd dumped Little Boy, but Pedro was there on Hermann Kapp's own request, so dumping him was ethically impossible. Even so, it would have been much better if the dead man had been Pedro instead of Al Simmonds. Simmonds could have opened any one of the cars which Hermann Kapp saw parked along the side streets, cars which he would have dearly liked to open himself using simple gadgets in his case. Hermann Kapp could in fact have picked the lock of almost any one of the cars, but he had never practised sufficiently to be quick about it, not like Al Simmonds. Spending ten minutes in the street opening up a car would be ridiculous. Besides, Kapp had his own way of stealing cars with no danger to it, provided he could find the kind of place he was looking for. But there was no multistorey car park, which was the best kind of place, nor did there seem to be much hope of finding one in these particular streets.

The police would soon be concentrating on this part of London. It would be difficult for them to seal off all the little streets, but not so difficult to blockade the main ones. Kapp's quick brain thought about holing up in one of the many small terrace houses in the side streets. Maybe they could find clean clothes in one of them. But it would mean killing the people there, and Kapp was

squeamish about that sort of thing. And besides that, the
police had Pedro's bag, and they also had Al Simmonds'
bag of course. There was no telling what Simmonds' bag
had in it. Now, more than ever, Kapp was anxious to
be away from Little Boy. It was ridiculous not to be taking
a risk with one of the cars, because they were taking a
big risk anyway. Everybody in London that night was
taking a big risk.

Then Kapp laughed out loud. Ahead of them was one
of the places the British called a "pub," a place where
much beer was drunk. Kapp knew all about the carelessness of people who frequent beer gardens and beer pal-
aces, and even "pubs," he had no doubt. In the parking
yard at the back of the pub it took but a couple of minutes
to find an unlocked car. The ignition switch was no problem. Being an electrical expert, Hermann Kapp could
manage that quickly enough. A minute later they were
out in the street, mobile again, with a registration number
not known to the police, at any rate, until the beer drinker
emerged from the pub. Even then the beer drinker would
stagger round for another half hour, slobbering on about
his lost car before he got round at last to telling the
police about it. Kapp reckoned he had a good hour before
he must change the car again. And in a good hour they
would be just where he wanted them to be, provided
he could read the map accurately. It all came down now
to reading the map correctly, and this he could do while
Anna Morgue drove the car. Pedro sprawled in the back
seat, making a knacker's yard out of it, Hermann Kapp
thought morosely to himself. He also thought Pedro was
being more than a bit inept, and not in any way measuring
up to his supposedly high reputation.

This judgement was unfair to the considerable abilities
of Abu l'Weifa, whose thoughts were currently occupied
with the problem of how he would dispose of Hermann

Kapp himself. To his Islamic mind, the woman was less of a problem. She was a woman wedded not to a man's prick but to a gun. A killer maybe—he had not yet forgotten the little Englishman—but Abu l'Weifa himself knew something of that part of the business. It was more the agile brain of the German which Abu l'Weifa feared. With the German gone, the bomb and its key would then be his. Abu l'Weifa saw no limit to the uses he and his particular friends might make of it.

Hermann Kapp took them first to the Old Kent Road. He decided to make a few miles as quickly as possible to the south. It was only fifteen minutes since they had ditched the van, and the police would still be sorting the position out. Once in the Old Kent Road headed southeast, he switched from a map of central London to one of greater London. Before reaching the main New Cross Road, he instructed Anna Morgue to take a small road off to the right, which eventually took them directly over the New Cross Road, to a place marked Telegraph Hill on his map. The route was then fairly easy for a little while, east for a mile on B2142, south for half a mile along B218, east for another mile along B236, then across the southward bound A21 into a still smaller road called Hither Green Lane, which in a mile or two became Northover and then Southover. Southover brought them to the much larger A2212, which they followed, but for only a third of a mile or so. Then Kapp directed them once again into a side road on the left. Here he lost precision, but after a mile or two he noticed the B265 roadsign, and the B265 was the road he now wanted. After three miles more they again reached a larger road, the A232, and again Kapp took them but a third of a mile along it, telling Anna Morgue once again to make a left turn into a much smaller country road. After perhaps a further mile the country road reached a largish copse, and there,

after pulling off onto a grass verge, they came to a stop.
It was a route which had scarcely given the police any
chance of intercepting them, and it had brought Hermann Kapp to just where he wanted to be. Map reading,
he decided, had its advantages. He felt infinitely easier
in his mind now, with Little Boy quite a distance away.
He looked across at Anna Morgue and thought to himself
that he was very nearly ready for his little game with
her.

London, Scotland Yard, 10:30 P.M.

If the case had been an ordinary one, Willy Best would
now have felt that he was close to breaking it. Once a
gang began to splinter, the job was usually three parts
done. True, the two members of the gang in his hands
were dead, but contrary to popular fallacy dead men
sometimes do tell tales, quite tall tales.

It had been a day of intense incident for Best himself
and for many others, the Commissioner, the Home Secretary, the newspapers, the government. But particularly
for Ernest Carruthers and for the two dead men. The
dead man found in the van, the van sprawled grotesquely
across the opposing traffic lanes of London Road, was a
new customer for Willy Best. An American, Albert Gar-
field Simmonds, if his papers were to be believed. But
international reports on Mr. Simmonds would soon be
flooding in, and Willy Best was making no speculations
until the evidence was in. Then there was a certain Pedro
Valesquez, for whom there were papers but no corpse.
Who the hell might this Pedro Valesquez be? Interesting,
particularly as information on that gentleman would also
soon be coming in. But of all the events of the day, the
most bizarre was the identity of the stiff, and he was
really becoming stiff, all right, they had found at 17A

Courtlane Mews. Who would have thought it? Mr. Sunion Webb, ex-M.P. Mr. Sunion Webb, just the kind of bloody awful character the police were always being forced to handle with kid gloves. The Soviets themselves Willy Best had some respect for. After all, they were only playing their own game, and why shouldn't they? It was the Sunion Webbs of this world who opened the floodgates of Willy Best's contempt. Men who sought to lay their own country low. Best felt he could kiss whoever it was who had done this job. And he guessed the Commissioner would be happy to follow suit—if somebody troubled to mention the idea to him.

But the thing which raised Best's spirits above all else was the size of the van they'd recovered from London Road. When he'd heard about the supposed furniture removal at 17A Courtlane Mews he'd conceived in his mind of a big van, the sort of van that might possibly have carried a plutonium bomb. The van in London Road was much too small for that. Willy Best had learned enough about nuclear weapons to know that plutonium had to be fired from all directions at high speed into an implosion configuration. He recalled that the Americans had referred to their first plutonium bomb as Big Boy, and now there were Big Boy hamburger joints all over the United States. He'd seen one himself during his brief trip to Washington. The van in London Road could never have accommodated Big Boy.

The Westminster Disaster

Downe, Kent, 5 A.M.

The night had been uneasy for Hermann Kapp and Anna
Morgue. Both had been strained and tired. Yet neither
had slept well. Each had nodded off fitfully from time
to time, Anna Morgue in the driver's seat of the stolen
car and Hermann Kapp in the nearby front passenger
seat. In an odd kind of way one seemed to sleep and
the other to be unable to sleep, almost as if they were
provoking each other to assault.

Daylight came, and Kapp, who was awake then, kept
glancing in a half-conscious way at the woman. She was
sleeping in the upright seat with her head thrown to
the right, her mouth open, and her auburn hair straggling
over the face. Thoughts began to move with their accus-
tomed quickness in Hermann Kapp's brain. Not remotely
as pretty as Susi, still asleep no doubt in her Darmstadt
flat. Not a thousandth part as pretty as Susi. So what was
there in it for him? Even as the question occurred to
him his penis began to rise tightly within his pants.

He was aware of a click from the back of the car. Pedro
had hauled himself with a grunt from the car, out into

the cool morning air. Pedro stretched himself nonchalantly, and then walked away along the edge of a ploughed field toward an isolated piece of woodland which stretched up one side of a domelike chalk hill. Hermann Kapp watched until Pedro was halfway up the hill, and then without wishing it, he dozed off.

A moment later, it seemed, he was awake. A glance at his watch showed that astonishingly he had slept for nearly thirty-five minutes. The time, 5:35, was still plenty early enough but Kapp had no wish for Pedro to go off by himself for half the day. Otherwise quite surely he would be off entirely by himself. Kapp had a sense of responsibility for his group as he had shown the previous evening, and so now he started reluctantly up the hill himself to give Pedro fair warning about the time.

Abu l'Weifa had known that Hermann Kapp would come after him. He had known it even as he had yawned in the morning air outside the car. There was a low hedge along the side of the ploughed field with a ripening crop of yellow wheat on the other side of it. Kapp noticed the wheat as he made his way steadily up the ploughed side of the hill. Why he noticed it he couldn't say, but it seemed to capture a moment of reality, like an impressionist painting. Then he came alongside the upper woodland, and Pedro was waiting for him there.

When he saw the knife in Pedro's hand, Kapp understood his strange unease throughout the night. When he saw the dark stain on the knife, he understood the gurgling death rattle from Al Simmonds. Then Abu l'Weifa asked him for the coded key to Little Boy, and Kapp also understood the thoughts in Abu l'Weifa's mind. Thankful that the man was not truly insane, that a motive existed for the knife and for the killing of Simmonds, Kapp explained about the key. He explained that the key had been set already, that Little Boy was open, open to the first correct radio frequency to be picked up with sufficient strength on his underwater antenna.

Abu l'Weifa took in this information slowly, and as he did so a dark, terrible fury swept through his mind and body. For now his power, the power of the bomb, the power of infinite blackmail, was gone from him. No power of decision over the bomb remained, not for anyone. The harsh musical chuckle came from deep in his throat as step by step Abu l'Weifa advanced on Hermann Kapp, and as he came on, Kapp became blindingly aware of his own true weakness. For Kapp now knew with a sharp certainty that he was desperately afraid, afraid both to kill and to be killed.

Abu l'Weifa came on slowly. He was in no hurry. Kapp retreated step by step before him. He watched with his gaze fixed on the knife blade. And Abu l'Weifa watched for the exact moment when the German would break, when he would turn, when he would attempt to run. In that moment, precisely as the German's back came round, the knife would be thrown with a force that would bury it to the hilt between the blades of Kapp's wide shoulders. Abu l'Weifa was aware of every detail of the German's retreat, but he was quite unaware of the continued rasping chuckle which emerged from his own throat.

Nor was Abu l'Weifa aware of Anna Morgue in the wheat field across the hedge, or of the heavy calibre bullet that ploughed its way into his body. Hermann Kapp heard the thud of it, and in the next four seconds he heard four more bullets bury themselves in Abu l'Weifa's heart, throat, and brain. The bullets came at exactly regular intervals, just as if Anna Morgue had been at rapid-fire practise on a target range.

Hermann Kapp found himself on the other side of the hedge. The freakish thought in his mind was that Abu l'Weifa had died without even the slightest sound emerging from his mouth. As his body had fallen to the ground there had been no twitch in it, nothing like the frenzied convulsions Kapp had seen before. It was as if his life had been instantaneously blotted out, by a dark, mysterious, cosmic shadow.

Anna Morgue was there waiting for him, the eyes fixed as he had seen them before. This time she did not need to order him to strip or to tie him down to the corner posts of a bed. Without seeking to resist her, he allowed his trousers to fall and voluntarily he sank onto the grass. She came on him with the strange-set eyes, with the light fleck in one of them, no more than an inch or two away from his own. His penis exploded the moment she took hold of it, and as the ejections came the eyes seemed to go on and on, boring deep into his mind. Then the woman was twisting herself, at first as if she had some control over what she was doing, and then more and more frenziedly. And now she was moaning and shouting, not whispering like the previous time. There were words to it, and Hermann Kapp realised with a shock that the words were a prayer, an Ave Marie.

The tenseness went out of the woman and the set look of her eyes was gone. Hermann Kapp had wondered several times what she'd looked like before, when she'd gone and locked herself away in the bathroom. Now he knew. She had a childlike beatific look, and her mouth had a wide-open smile that he had never seen before.

They started down the side of the wheat field, with Hermann Kapp going ahead. When they reached the car he turned and Anna Morgue had lost the beatific look. The fit and the following trance had gone, and she was normal again, as near as she would ever be to normality.

It was 7:15 A.M. when Hermann Kapp started the car. In not much more than a mile he came to a village.

Stopping there beside a public telephone booth, he took a small notebook from his case, checked a number, went into the booth, lifted the receiver, and dialled. A flat male voice told him that he was speaking to the Metropolitan Police. First he asked if he could be heard clearly, and on being assured by the voice that he could, Hermann Kapp said that the bomb, taken from 17A Courtlane Mews on the previous afternoon, was now in the Thames river at the bottom of a slipway one-third—he repeated, one-third—of a mile below Waterloo Bridge. The slipway, he said, opened to the river off Barge House Street, and the lane which ran to the slipway had an iron gate across it. The flat voice at the other end asked him to repeat the message, and Kapp immediately replaced the phone in its cradle. If the police did not make automatic recordings of such calls, they were bigger fools than Kapp took them for.

Driving west now for nearly two miles, they reached the A233, and north for another mile along the A233 brought them to a small airport. The police were not fools, and neither was Hermann Kapp. A car stolen from the vicinity of the street where the van and the corpse of Al Simmonds had been so spectacularly abandoned would be a matter of particular suspicion. Had Kapp been a policeman himself he would assuredly have put out a special alert about that stolen car. So while he had thought it safe enough to drive early in the morning along small country lanes, Hermann Kapp had no intention of driving into the airport itself. About five hundred yards away he pulled the car off the road onto a track which led through a gate into a field. Anna Morgue opened the gate and he drove through. Kapp's last touch to the car was to open up the bonnet. From his case he then took out a clean shirt, for the shirt he was wearing had a noticeable red stain on it. It took but a moment to make the change, and then carrying the case, he and Anna Morgue walked the remaining five hundred yards to the airfield.

Hermann Kapp did not believe he had left anything obviously identifiable behind him at 17A Courtlane Mews, nor did he think Anna Morgue had either—when she was in her usual state, as she seemed to be nearly all the time, the woman was a thoroughly efficient operator. Hermann Kapp had always been easy in his mind on that score, otherwise he would never have brought her into this affair. There would be fingerprints at 17A Courtlane Mews, but so long as the police did not know their identity, fingerprints would be useless. But were the police unaware of their identity? Somebody with a long arm might very well have been talking discreetly with the police. From the moment Sunion Webb had been shot this possibility had bulked large in the mind of Hermann Kapp. If it were not for this possibility, he and Anna Morgue would simply have taken a train to the south coast and then boarded a cross-channel ferry.

So the charter flight, all arranged in the papers Sunion Webb had given to him, interested Hermann Kapp. The same long arm would surely have been at work on that charter flight, but with a gun in the hand of Anna Morgue a small airfield was not a particularly formidable place. The attraction, of course, of a small aircraft was that it could fly under the British radar screen. Once they were in the air there would be no customs, no immigration, no police.

Kapp had given some considerable thought to where he would direct the charter plane. He had known since boyhood the almost deserted north coastal regions of German Friesland, and this area, he decided, would suit him excellently. Of a certainty, the second half of the two million Swiss francs would not be paid now, but with two of the four of them dead, his own share would be exactly the same as it would have been in the original arrangement. Odd, the way things worked out.

Kapp put a stop to this vacuous wandering of his mind. The airport buildings had no great size about them, the sort of place you could look around in a couple of minutes, the sort of place where an experienced eye could easily spot a deviation from normal routine, like having half a dozen policemen distributed around the place. Kapp could have picked out such a situation in an instant. He could have picked it out in the eyes of a woman sweeping the floor, or in the cafeteria staff, or in the movements of airport officials who came in and out of the building. There being nothing to trouble him, he told Anna Morgue to get herself a cup of coffee at the cafeteria. Then he strolled off by himself with the intention of discovering the whereabouts of the charter company, Pengelly Charter. Within a moment he was back at the cafeteria because the woman sweeping the floor gave him an immediate answer to his query about Pengelly Charter by simply pointing to a coloured man sitting there not far from Anna Morgue. The fellow Kapp could see was eating a large plate of bacon and eggs. So Kapp bought himself a coffee and sat down beside Anna Morgue.

Julian John Marquette was keenly aware of the two strangers, the stringy woman and the fair man. He guessed the fair man to be watching him from behind those big tinted glasses.

Julian John Marquette had been told three days earlier by his manager to report for an 8 A.M. charter flight, the party being of four persons, sexes unspecified. But when he himself had arrived at the airport at 7 A.M. that morning, the manager telephoned to say the charter was off, except that if anyone should happen to turn up for it he, Marquette, was to report back immediately. It was just another of those mysterious situations which Julian John had experienced before, the situations he didn't like.

And here were two people who had evidently turned up for the flight. Marquette knew it to be so even before the man in the tinted glasses came over the few yards which separated their tables. The man spoke to him about the flight, showing him the charter papers which were all perfectly in order. Still, he had his instructions, and Julian John thought he'd better do as he'd been told. So he took the man and woman out from the airport building into the morning sunshine. It was about a two-hundred-yard walk along the concrete perimeter road to the Pengelly office, to the area where the company's three small planes usually stood overnight. Two of them were there now, one a Piper which Julian John would use for the charter, if indeed the charter were still on. Outside the Pengelly office, which was simply a small isolated hut, he asked about the other two members of the party. The man with the tinted glasses said that they had been detained and would not be coming. Thinking that maybe this was the real reason for the stopping and changing of the arrangements, Julian John went into the office to explain the situation to his manager.

Hermann Kapp had a profound dislike of having his whereabouts reported. With no apparent danger in the airport, and with the Piper standing there rather obviously ready for takeoff, he saw no reason why this pilot should be permitted the luxury of making a telephone call, if that indeed was what he had gone into the office to do. So with a slight flick of his head to Anna Morgue he followed the man into the hut. Sure enough, the man had a phone in his hand and was just beginning to make a call.

Julian John Marquette was in the process of dialling

when he saw them come into the room. If the fair-headed man had been pointing a gun he would not have been very greatly surprised. From the nature of some of the charters he'd done for Pengelly, it would have figured. But it was the woman who was holding the gun, and this was something that went outside his imagination, particularly the steadiness of the hand which held the gun. Not a hand to rock the cradle with, a philosopher might have thought. But Julian John Marquette was not a philosopher and contented himself with replacing the receiver. The woman's own eyes had a look of their own which effectively dissuaded him from trying a thrust at the arm holding the gun.

Marquette had no clear option but to allow himself to be marched out to the Piper. The woman swung herself into the seat immediately behind him, and her companion took the co-pilot's seat. They allowed him to warm up the engines. Pity he hadn't just managed to put through the call as he'd been told to do. He'd kept his job by obeying orders. He taxied the Piper onto the runway, and in a couple of minutes more they were airborne.

Hermann Kapp waited until they were about fifteen hundred feet up. Then he ordered the pilot to hand over the controls. There were very few things which Kapp couldn't do in a general unspecialised way. He was not an experienced pilot and would have had trouble with an awkward landing, particularly when there were updrafts. Yet in his head he knew how to do it all, so there was no real difficulty for him in managing the controls once they were in the air. Probably he could have managed the Piper entirely by himself, but he had rejected the idea for several reasons. He just might have muffed the takeoff. The control tower might have seen something wrong. And the pilot would have had to be scrubbed, another killing.

Central London, 7:30 A.M.

Hermann Kapp had been right. The call he'd made just after 7:15 A.M. had indeed been recorded by the Metropolitan Police. It had been quickly typed and it was soon in front of Willy Best. It was not a lone message, however. More than two score of telephone messages, all purporting to be bomb disclosures, had come in during the night. A good half of all the calls had already been traced. Most of the callers had been loquacious, and it had been easy while the telephone circuits were open to determine the whereabouts of the bloody fools who were seeking to attract notice to themselves.

Best instantly picked out Kapp's message as one of the few to be taken seriously, even though he still believed that a plutonium bomb would have been too large in size to have been removed from 17A Courtlane Mews. The fact that Hermann Kapp had spoken slowly and clearly, that he had wasted no words, that he had broken circuit as soon as his message was completed, pointed in Willy Best's estimation to a dangerous nut. The foreign accent, German, the telephone operator had thought, was another indication. Ordinary German tourists were not given to making false calls to the police.

And the message itself had an ominous quality about it. Willy Best had thought about where he himself would put such a bomb. He'd spent half the night thinking about it. He'd allowed himself to become mesmerised by "safe houses," because obviously you could hardly leave a thing like that sitting around in the street. He'd had his men combing the multistorey car parks, and combing the parking areas around the residential squares in central London. But the river hadn't occurred to him. Yet the river was quite a place for such a thing. It might stay there for a year and never be noticed. It could be set off just when you were ready to set it off, Best thought to himself without realising how very close he had now come to Hermann Kapp's reason for making the telephone call.

Best decided the 7:15 message was important enough for him to take a look for himself. It was after 8:45, however, before the chain of three police cars with Best in the lead car reached Waterloo Bridge. The cars followed the route driven the previous evening by Anna Morgue, left off Waterloo Road into Stamford Road, then left again past the Stationary Office into Upper Ground. The police knew of two lanes which led to the river, and it was in the first where they found the iron gate. It took them longer than Al Simmonds had taken to get the gate open, because the police had to scout around to find someone who could unlock it. A man in a cloth cap and shirt sleeves, muttering imprecations against the bloody fuzz, came at last. It was nearing 9:10 by the time Willy Best reached the river's edge.

The iron gate and the slipway were there, just as the message had said. It was now that the German accent became very significant. A south London accent would have meant nothing at all, but what German merely trying out a hoax would know of a place like this? As he stopped to examine the slipway, Willy Best's heart was thudding in his ears. The place had the right smell about it, he thought. A heavy object had recently gone down the slipway. Slight markings went down the slipway, more or less to the low water mark. A few days of being covered repeatedly by the tides would have greened them up, and since they weren't yet greened they must have been made recently. QED, Willy Best thought to himself.

He told his men to question the people in the surrounding warehouses, to find when the slipway had last been used, and for what purpose. Then squatting down close to the water itself, and staring down into the almost opaque green depths, he saw a glint of bright metal. When the pulley block had come loose of the eye in the van, when Little Boy had rolled free for a while before reaching the water, the binding of the surrounding carpeting had been loosened, permitting Little Boy to slide bodily inside the roll of the carpet. This freedom of movement had led to about eight inches of steel cylinder emerging from one of the ends of the carpet, and it was this projecting metal that Willy Best could now see. He called the driver of one of the cars to look with him, and after staring for a while, the driver also picked out the glint of Little Boy.

Nothing was proved yet, Best understood full well. But by now he'd got all the supporting evidence he needed to call out a full investigating squad. He still didn't believe in a nuclear bomb, but there was certainly something down there in the river to be looked into. He jumped into the lead car and picked up a microphone, calculating in his mind how long it would take for the divers to collect their equipment, and for them to fight their way through the London morning traffic. An hour, maybe an hour and a half, he thought.

Hermann Kapp's message had said what he wanted to say both simply and accurately. But it had not said that the coded key to the bomb in the Thames river was open. Nor was it said that the radio frequency to which the bomb detonator was tuned had been adjusted to the frequency used that week by the Special Branch of the Metropolitan Police. To prevent detonation from other police messages that were being sent back and forth through London, Hermann Kapp had also set a high radio intensity for the detonator, such as could come only from a transmission made at the site of the bomb itself. And he had chosen Barge House Street, the lane with the iron gate and the slipway on the south side of the Thames River, as a place from which a police transmission could hardly be made by accident. It would be made from there only when he, Hermann Kapp, was ready for it to be made.

Willy Best knew nothing of these things, or in the moment he pressed the transmitter switch, of anything else at all.

Whitehall, the seat of government through the centuries, was less than a mile away from the seemingly remote slipway that Hermann Kapp had chosen so carefully. Many of the buildings of Whitehall were old, built in stonework now in poor condition. With the explosion of Little Boy they came down like so many rotten fruit. They had seen ages of strong government, ages of great glory, but in the end they had seen a nation top to bottom, with the feeble at the top and the more virile in subservience, a nation that had largely lost the collective will to survive.

Holland, 9:17 A.M.

Hermann Kapp's navigational plan for reaching the north German coast was straightforward, merely to fly northeast until they hit the Dutch coast, then to fly along the coastal margin, north and east along the chain of Dutch islands to the mouth of the Ems. With a strong following wind they had reached the Dutch coast near Haarlem just before 9:15.

Kapp was thinking his course had dipped a little too far into the Dutch mainland when the flash came. The flash was almost two hundred miles away, yet it was still bright enough to leave an afterimage in the eyes. Kapp put the Piper into a gentle climb and turned to his left, toward London. It took astonishingly little time, less than a minute, it seemed, for a vastly extending brilliant flat cloud to appear on the distant horizon. Kapp looked squarely into the eyes of the woman close behind him there, and saw in them that the "something" between them had at last been resolved.

Julian John Marquette saw in the exultant faces of his two unwanted passengers, in their foam-flecked lips and widened nostrils, that these people were mad, demented, insane. He also saw that the scare story he had read about in the papers was no scare story at all. It was the truth, and these people beside him had to do with it. His wife and daughter were inside London in that explosion, and a light exploded in his head, much more furiously than any afterimage in the eyes. There was nothing he could do to guide the plane, otherwise he would instantly have thrown it into the worst loops and acrobatic contortions of which he was capable. But there was just one important thing he could do. Marquette leant forward and pressed the switches which cut out the engines. As their roar died, Anna Morgue shot him in the back of the head.

The plane was still moving upward, but now without engine power it stalled immediately and began turning like a falling leaf. Had it not been for the lingering after-image in his eyes, Hermann Kapp might still have done something to stop the endless turning, the turning that prevented him from moving the way he wanted to go. He was still fighting to hold back the inert body of Julian John Marquette, and still fighting to reach the engine switches, in the instant that the plane hit the ground.

ROCKETS IN URSA MAJOR

'Embedded in it somewhere is a curiously attractive, almost poetic quality.'
The Listener

'There is enough Hoyle ingenuity to tempt oldies to stay tuned.'
The Sunday Times

SEVEN STEPS TO THE SUN

'Another Fred and Geoffrey Hoyle leap into the future that's as readable and racy as anything they've done.' *Daily Mail*

'This is a remarkable story, well-told, and too credible for comfort.'
The Listener

FIFTH PLANET

'A tense adventure sandwiched between two slivers of higher maths. . . . A very well told story this, with some nice touches of political prediction.'
The Daily Telegraph

THE INFERNO

'Aficionados will be reverently delighted by the expert display of hard science and maths used in the preliminary investigation. . . . Here is entertainment and instruction in high-level astrophysics all in one package.'
The Sunday Times

INTO DEEPEST SPACE

'. . . this further account of Dick Warboys in full cry after the elusive Yela emerges as the most moving, poetic idea the Hoyles have so far delineated; the inverse universe concept is given human definition.'
The Times